COCHISE
OF ARIZONA

COCHISE
OF ARIZONA

Oliver La Farge

Illustrated
by
L. F. Bjorklund

New Foreword
by
Marc Simmons
and
An Appreciation by John Pen La Farge

SANTA FE

Sunstone books may be purchased for educational, business, or sales promotional use.
For information please write: Special Markets Department, Sunstone Press,
P.O. Box 2321, Santa Fe, New Mexico 87504-2321.
Printed on acid-free paper
∞

Library of Congress Cataloging-in-Publication Data

La Farge, Oliver, 1901-1963.
  Cochise of Arizona / by Oliver La Farge ; illustrated by L.F. Bjorklund ; new foreword by
Marc Simmons ; and an appreciation by John Pen La Farge.
    pages cm. -- (Southwest heritage series)
  Summary: A fictionalized biography of Cochise who, aided by his friend and interpreter
Tom Jeffords, works hard to negotiate a peace treaty between white men and his people, the
Chiricahua Apaches.
  ISBN 978-0-86534-675-8 (softcover : alk. paper)
  1. Cochise, Apache chief, 1805?-1874--Juvenile fiction. [1. Cochise, Apache chief,
1805?-1874--Fiction. 2. Chiricahua Indians--Fiction. 3. Indians of North America--South-
west, New--Fiction. 4. Southwest, New--History--1848---Fiction.] I. Bjorklund, Lorence
F., illustrator. II. Title.
  PZ7.L138Co 2014
  [Fic]--dc23
                              2013046796

WWW.SUNSTONEPRESS.COM
SUNSTONE PRESS / POST OFFICE BOX 2321 / SANTA FE, NM 87504-2321 /USA
(505) 988-4418 / ORDERS ONLY (800) 243-5644 / FAX (505) 988-1025

ISBN 978-1-63293-582-3

CONTENTS

I

THE SOUTHWEST HERITAGE SERIES

II

FOREWORD TO THIS EDITION
by
Marc Simmons

III

AN APPRECIATION OF A FATHER
by
John Pen La Farge

IV

OLIVER LA FARGE
(1901–1963)
by
Edith Bayles Ricketson

V

COCHISE OF ARIZONA

SOUTHWEST HERITAGE SERIES

I

THE SOUTHWEST HERITAGE SERIES

"The past is not dead. In fact, it's not even past."
—William Faulkner, Requiem for a Nun

The history of the United States is written in hundreds of regional histories and literary works. Those letters, essays, memoirs, biographies and even collections of fiction are often first-hand accounts by people who wanted to memorialize an event, a person or simply record for posterity the concerns and issues of the times. Many of these accounts have been lost, destroyed or overlooked. Some are in private or public collections but deemed to be in too fragile condition to permit handling by contemporary readers and researchers.

However, now with the application of twenty-first century technology, nineteenth and twentieth century material can be reprinted and made accessible to the general public. These early writings are the DNA of our history and culture and are essential to understanding the present in terms of the past.

The Southwest Heritage Series is a form of literary preservation. Heritage by definition implies legacy and these early works are our legacy from those who have gone before us. To properly present and preserve that legacy, no changes in style or contents have been made. The material reprinted stands on its own as it first appeared. The point of view is that of the author and the era in which he or she lived. We would not expect photographs of people from the past to be re-imaged with modern clothes, hair styles and backgrounds. We should not, therefore, expect their ideas and personal philosophies to reflect our modern concepts.

Remember, reading their words and sharing their thoughts is a passport back into understanding how the past was shaped and how it influenced today's world.

Our hope is that new access to these older books will provide readers with a challenging and exciting experience.

Oiver La Farge as a young man. *Photograph courtesy of John Pen La Farge Archives*

II

FOREWORD TO THIS EDITION

by
Marc Simmons

"Indian Man"
The Santa Fe Reporter, February 1, 1979

When he died in the summer of 1963, Santa Fe author Oliver Hazard Perry La Farge was already ranked among the literary lions of Southwestern letters. Since that time his reputation has continued to grow and new honors have been added to his name. One of the most fitting tributes came when Santa Fe decided to name a new branch library after him.

The matter was attended by some controversy, partly because almost nothing that transpires in New Mexico's capital escapes heated debate, but partly too because Oliver La Farge was the kind of man who generated argument. His friend, the poet Winfield Townley Scott, once characterized him as "an aristocratic Yankee, a man of fierce pride who held his opinions strongly."

La Farge was much enamored of Santa Fe's Old World charm, as many other people of sensitivity and imagination have been. But his was not the usual quiet admiration for the place. He campaigned openly and with energy to keep crass commercialism and tasteless modernity at bay.

With support of like-minded citizens, he helped organize the Old Santa Fe Association and was a leader in getting a Historic Zoning Ordinance enacted. And in his weekly column, "The Santa Fe Bird Watcher," published for many years in *The Santa Fe New Mexican*, he repeatedly flailed away at the up-to-date boomers who were ready, at the drop of a dollar, to do away with what he called "the town's native style, unpretentious, priceless and vitally important."

In this respect, Oliver La Farge was more than a little out of step with contemporary America. He took a firm stand against the mindless doctrine of "change for change's sake" upon which so many of our social and economic premises continue to be based. Particularly in the fields of art and architecture, he noted, "nothing is more deadly than the innovations of the incompetent seeking to be striking." In condemning phoniness, fads and "daring new departures cooked up much as women's clothes designers and hairdressers cook up new styles for the fair sex," he stepped on toes.

When time came to choose a name for Santa Fe's branch library, more than fifteen years after La Farge's death, there were those who remembered and who objected to bestowing this honor upon him. Their complaints appeared in the press: Oliver La Farge lacked vision, he opposed progress, he was archaic, preoccupied with the past.

Unfortunately, the subject of attack was not around to defend himself, but others were ready to take up the cudgel in his behalf. Ultimately the Library Board decided to go ahead with its original intention, gracing the new branch with La Farge's name—on the basis of literary merit.

The man around whom this brief tempest in a teapot had swirled wore a number of hats in his tenure of 61 years: those of field anthropologist, linguist, professor, journalist, Indian advocate, lieutenant colonel in the Army Air Command during World War II, and editor. But it was in the area of literature that Oliver La Farge made his largest mark and won enduring fame. He was a writer to his fingertips and a lover of books to his shoe soles.

His first published volume put his name in lights before he was 30. The book was *Laughing Boy*, a novel of Navajo life, and it won the Pulitzer Prize in 1930. The background for the work La Farge had collected when, as an anthropology student at Harvard in the mid-1920s, he participated in summer archeological expeditions to the Navajo Reservation. From this experience he drew more than literary material. He gained a love for the Southwest and a sympathy for the Indian and his problems that were to prove a focus for his life thereafter.

Born of old New England stock and numbering the 19th century naval heroes Commodores Oliver Hazard Perry and Matthew Perry among his ancestors, La Farge also had a dash of Indian blood in his veins. Upon him, this slight aboriginal strain left a strong imprint. Owing to his dark complexion and craggy features, his mother affectionately nicknamed him "Indian Man."

After the success of *Laughing Boy* and the appearance of several scholarly works on the Mayan people of southern Mexico and Guatemala, Oliver La Farge was firmly established in the public mind as "an authority on Indians." A string of books on Native Americans that followed served to reinforce the image. His reputation, as well as his temperament and reforming tendencies, led him, perhaps inevitably, to become a champion of Indian rights and an exposer of abuses against them.

By the 1930s he was actively involved in the thankless and, as of then, unpopular work of Indian defense organizations. For many years he served as president and guiding spirit of the New York-based American Association on Indian Affairs. It was a cause that engaged him most of his adult life.

Just a short time before his death, already having trouble breathing, he drove the 80 miles from Santa Fe to Taos to confer with Indian leaders regarding the ongoing struggle to recover their sacred Blue Lake from the National Forest Service. Here was a moral issue to which he had long devoted his energies, and one whose successful conclusion he would not live to see.

Before the new spirit of the 1970s ushered in respect for Indian ways and culture, people who spoke out on their behalf were often subject to rough handling. La Farge tells in his autobiographical *Raw Material*, published in 1945, how he fared when subpoenaed to testify before the Senate Indian Affairs Committee in Washington.

Beforehand, his stomach churned and he could not even drink a cup of coffee. He knew all too well what pressure the senators could place on witnesses. During his testimony he relates, "I was taken beautifully to pieces." The same fate befell other pro-Indian witnesses who "went down in agony."

The Committee chairman, La Farge contends, was ruthless and sometimes unbelievably rude. "The more I heard, the sicker and angrier I felt. I think any American will get angry, regardless of which side he is on, when a senator starts working over a perfectly sincere witness."

The comments were typical of Oliver La Farge. The strong sense of justice that weighed upon him kept him fighting. His courage sustained him. The Indians whom he had befriended and whose battles he had waged knew that he was one white man who could be trusted. At his open gravesite a delegation of Pueblos unashamedly wept.

While it was in the area of Indian history and literature that La Farge won his reputation, it bears mentioning that he produced one fine book on New Mexico's Hispanic population. At the Santa Fe Fiesta in 1936, he had met Consuelo Baca, destined to become his wife. She was a member of one of the old aristocratic families, the Bacas having been prime movers in the politics and economy of New Mexico for generations.

Hearing from his wife of the traditional life she had known as a child on the Baca ranch high in the Sangre de Cristos, La Farge set down in his *Behind the Mountains* a lyrical account of a way of life that had vanished. While it received no Pulitzer Prize like *Laughing Boy,* it nevertheless earned the affection of New Mexicans, who continue to regard the book as a regional classic.

Santa Fe has changed a great deal—more than most people are prepared to acknowledge—since Oliver La Farge died in August 1963. The small-town atmosphere with "its warmth and rewards" he often spoke of and admired is swiftly becoming a thing of the past. But with his name appropriately enshrined over the doorway of a library, perhaps the Modern Age will not be inclined to forget his love for the city and for the people of the Southwest.

III

AN APPRECIATION OF A FATHER
by
John Pen La Farge

It is difficult to know what to say when people ask about my father's career. The person asking has usually discovered an aspect of Father's career that had previously been unknown to him, which presents a puzzlement. The question, however reasonable, is not easily answered.

My father had a varied and complicated set of interests and talents which led him into a life of multiple careers, most of which he practiced simultaneously.

Oliver La Farge (b. 1901) was the scion of a number of old and important families of the East coast. The La Farges, per se, were far and away the most recently arrived. They had been royalist plantation owners who had escaped the Haitian revolt of the early 1800s. One family tradition has it that Jean Frédéric de La Farge became a favorite of the mistresses of the leader of the revolt, Toussaint L'Ouverture, and they helped him to escape the island.

In the United States, Jean Frédéric became successful in the import business in New Orleans, then Philadelphia, then invested in real estate in Louisiana and, also, founded a settlement that is yet known as LaFargeville in upper-state New York.

Other of Father's non-La Farge ancestors were Roger Williams, who founded Rhode Island as the first colony formed on the principle of religious freedom; Benjamin Franklin; both Commodores Perry—Matthew, who opened Japan in 1854, and Oliver Hazard, the "Hero of Lake Erie," for whom Father was named; and John La Farge, one of America's premier artists of the second half of the nineteenth century, an early visitor to Tahiti and to Japan (opened by his Uncle-in-law Matthew Perry), and who was, also, a major creative force who developed many new stained-glass techniques, including opalescent stained glass.

Father developed an early interest in the American Indians, partly from his father, the architect Christopher Grant La Farge, who had deep respect for their knowledge of nature and hunting, and who used Indian guides and canoers on hunting and fishing trips in Canada. Grant was, evidently, quite the expert with guns and fishing rod. Due to this abiding interest on Father's part (and due to his somewhat-Indian features, with high-cheekbones, dark hair, and feet that pointed straight forward), he was called, "Indian Man" by his mother, Florence Bayard Lockwood La Farge. It seems likely, as well, that his interest in the outdoors and those who enjoy its life was encouraged by Theodore Roosevelt, a good friend of the family's. Certainly, Roosevelt influenced Father's choice of anthropology as his life's work when he favorably reviewed Henry Fairfield Osborn's book, *Men of the Old Stone Age*, which fascinated Father.

Another friend of the family, and a cousin, Owen Wister, had gone west and also wrote about the West, so one may say that Father was surrounded by Western influences throughout his early life.

Grant's love of the outdoors was considerable, and he knew and admired Indians east, north, and in the Southwest. Indeed, he produced both drawings and paintings for anthropologist Elsie Clews Parsons's book, *American Indian Life*, and he spent considerable time with her on her expeditions to the Southwest.

As an undergraduate student at Harvard, Father majored in anthropology. Consequently, as a student he came out to New Mexico during the summers of the early twenties. New Mexico appealed greatly to him, and he became especially fond of the Navajos, whose sense of ruggedness and individuality greatly appealed to him.

His interest in the Southwest came as something of a surprise to him. Until he entered Harvard, anthropology, to him, had meant the Old World, partly because he had been entranced by *Men of the Old Stone Age* and like works. When he entered Harvard he discovered the university had a number of professors who knew much of American anthropology and who greatly influenced its future by re–directing their students' attention to America. Most famous among them, perhaps, was Alfred M. Tozzer, to whom Grant made certain his son was introduced soon after entering college. At least one of Father's biographers believes Grant pushed Father in this direction in order to continue, vicariously, his own fascination with Indians, and it was soon after this that Grandfather was commissioned by Parsons to illustrate her book.

Because of his work in the Southwest, during his time at Harvard, Father decided his interest lay not with the archeological branch of anthropology, but, rather, with the living branch, with ethnology, the study of culture and the distribution of culture.

Another engagement of that time was the nation-wide interest in the Bursum Bill. Protectors of Indian rights and Indian interests everywhere were outraged by a bill introduced in 1922 by New Mexico senator Holm Bursum. In effect, the bill would have legalized squatters' rights and the squatters' diversion of water for farming. Now, this sounds innocent enough without context, but in New Mexico, over centuries, both Spanish-Americans and, later, Anglos had moved onto Indian land and had used Indian water, squatting, sometimes for many years. As the Pueblo Indians had, from time immemorial, sought the best land, that is, the richest and most productive land, the temptation to squat must have been almost unbearable, especially as the Indians had little recourse.

At the behest of friends and interested parities, Senator Bursum had introduced his bill to make legal and permanent his supporters' claims. Immediately, the bill was opposed by all Indian rights groups, the two largest of which, the National Association on Indian Affairs and John Collier's Indian Defense Association, were joined into the Association on American Indian Affairs. Father was convinced to become its president, a position he held on and off until his death in 1963.

The Bursum Bill was eventually defeated and, in its stead, was passed a bill which set up a board that adjudicated all claims to land, fairly. Thereby, Bursum and his supporters received almost exactly the opposite of what they had wanted.

Father was one of a new kind of White interested in Indian matters. Before, there had been an assumption, both spoken and unspoken, that the Indian was a man on his way out, that his civilization was dying and would inevitably die, completely. Thereby, the government's policy, and that of Indian protectors, had been to assimilate the Indian into White culture as well and as completely as possible. With the 1920s, Father, and others, began to hope that Indian culture would not vanish, but could be preserved or, even, encouraged to grow healthy, again.

His twenties archaeological expeditions to New Mexico gradually began to shift Father's focus from the pre-historic Anasazi Indian to contemporary and living cultures, even as his Harvard Hemenway fellowship paid for his archaeological interests. So it was. He decided to change his focus from the archeology to ethnology, the investigation of culture.

Father's change was followed by a master's degree, and its thesis,

"Derivation of the Apache and Navajo Culture," in 1929, these two cultures being related by language.

Nevertheless, his interest in archaeology remained and resulted in several expeditions to central America, beginning in 1925, with Frans Blom, to study the Maya for the Carnegie Institution. Blom was another young Harvard Mayanist. Blom did the archaeological research on their journeys, while Father researched the Mayan languages, studying which language derived from which and their possible relationship to the Mayan hieroglyphs, many of which are untranslated to this day. The expedition was written up in *Tribes and Temples*, the first of father's three anthropological books on his Mayan work. It was during this expedition that Father found an Olmec head, one of his proudest moments.

One of the more familiar artifacts of Central America are the gargantuan heads, made by the Olmecs, a prehistoric Mexican culture. They are some 10 feet tall, made of black basalt, and feature a head with thick lips and wearing a helmet. Once thought to have been ball players, current theory is that they are the memorial heads of rulers.

In his work in Mesoamerica, as well as in his work with the Indians of the Southwest, especially the Navajo, Father demonstrated the same ability to make friends and to make people comfortable as had been demonstrated by his grandfather, John, during his travels to the South Pacific and to Japan. Both men had the ability to put people at their ease by treating everyone as equals, as not foreigners or as strange people "over there," but, rather, as though they were worthy of trust, no matter what their social station.

An example bears out this assertion. In Guatemala, Father and Doug Beyers, another Harvard anthropologist, stopped at a ranch for food and shelter. The ranch manager, a Ladino (and, thus, of a lower caste), told them he was sorry, but, not having been warned, he had, "nothing in the house."

Father wrote, "Barring this we lived like kings. . . he himself put off a business trip so as to guide us. . . his wife, without being asked, went through our packs and washed all our dirty clothes. . ."

D'Arcy McNickle, one of Father's biographers, goes on to quote from *The Door in the Wall*, a short anthropological story, "Ethnology," one character says, "is a slow process of gaining acceptance. And if you don't gain acceptance? You just go on being friendly with everyone, even the ones you would like to haul off and kick in the butt."

I stress this characteristic, as it played so much of a part in my own up-bringing. Santa Fe, Northern New Mexico, really, is a naturally diverse place where, especially in the first half of the twentieth century, one lived an "inclusive" life, perforce. There was no choice in the matter, except the choice to live in New Mexico. This life of "diversity" was not a matter of politics or of being politically correct; it was not a matter of rhetoric.

Protestant Anglos lived cheek by jowl with Catholic Spanish-Americans. The Indians, although they lived on the pueblos (rarely in-town, until recently), were an object of fascination. Not to be interested in two exotic cultures whose traditions and languages lived on, despite their being under stress, was to miss the larger part of why one lived in New Mexico. It was considered insane.

This feeling, this understanding, has changed, now, but its import does not change.

Thereby, I was the product of a mixed marriage (as yet unusual), Protestant Anglo with a Catholic Spanish-American, Consuelo Otile Baca. Father's living was largely made from his dedication to writing, but also from his dedication to the Indians and to their welfare. I was brought up, necessarily, with appreciation of the famed "three cultures," nor would my parents have had it any other way.

This meant that I went to grade school with the widest range of children. Today, Santa Fe is considerably divided by income, and, thereby, the old style of family-compound living, traditional to the Spanish, is going by the boards, and so is the heterogeneity of the neighborhoods. Then, my school had children whose parents were wealthy, were poets or artists, were businessmen, or investors in uranium mines, or mad scientists; likewise, there were children whose parents were the poorest of the poor, were plumbers, or butchers, or unskilled workers.

Aside from an invaluable non-academic education, I gained quite an insight into people, into people of different cultures, and into what one must necessarily tolerate.

This last was one of the more constant lessons of my childhood. My father, especially, balanced my fundamental and inescapable understanding of his upper-class background and of my mother's aristocratic New Mexican family with an understanding that the poor Spanish-Americans around us and at school had worth in proportion to their character, not according to their pocketbooks. More (and to my father, deeper) the Indians—who were poor to the extent of having neither running water nor electricity—were people he admired deeply and fervently, and he stressed that their nobility transcended any consideration of class.

In 1926, Father joined Blom in the recently created Department of Middle-American Research at Tulane University, where he wrote monographs on subjects such as the syncretistic Guatemalan religion (an unusual combination of their ancient shaman–based religion with an over-layer of Catholicism) and commissioned such artifacts as a purpose-made Navajo saddle for the museum, while continuing his research into the Mayan language.

New Orleans was the proverbial eye-opener for Father. There he discovered another kind of person entirely: artistic, bohemian, creative, outside of the east-coast upper class, outside of the main-stream of American society, as well. These people gave him a sense of what was possible in life if one did not have to conform to bourgeois American expectations or to any expectations, altogether. This discovery shaped a good deal of his life from that point forward, culminating in his permanent move to Santa Fe, just before World War II (a move interrupted only by war service).

In New Orleans, he met and socialized with such people as William Saroyan, William Faulkner, Sherwood Anderson, Noel Coward, artists Enrique Alfarez, Caroline Durieux, and Angela Gregory, and Bill Spratling. The first four were writers of great note. Spratling was an architecture professor at Tulane, who went to Mexico and, as a designer of jewelry and silver, revivified the creative spirit and silver industry of Taxco. His designs and his studio are, even today, major influences on Mexican design.

In 1930, Father became a board member, later president of the organization that eventually became the Association on American Indian Affairs. With this move, Father became permanently committed to more than an anthropological interest in the Indians, but also, to fighting for Indian rights and welfare, professionally.

It must also be said that Father's interest in Indian rights was encouraged by example within the family. His uncle John, Grant's youngest brother, a Jesuit priest, had committed himself to racial relations and anti-racism early in the twentieth century. Indeed, Fr. John's writings on racism were so well appreciated that he was commissioned by Pope Pius XI, along with two other Jesuits, to write an encyclical condemning racism, in general, and anti-Semitism, in particular. Unhappily, the encyclical was never promulgated due to Pius XI's death in 1939.

Fr. John's example stood before Father as a guide as to how one might live one's life so as to realize one's moral values in concrete fashion.

During the twenties and thirties, among his activities on behalf of the Indians, Father composed the first Navajo alphabet and, with John Collier (later Commissioner of Indian Affairs under Franklin Delano Roosevelt), composed a constitution for the Hopi tribes, one which, I believe, they have not, yet, ratified.

Because of his anthropological work, Father's interest in creative writing was relegated to a secondary role, although one of his short stories, "North is Black," was chosen for a collection, *Best American Short Stories for 1927*.

However, this creative outlet for his imagination was too valuable to be let go by the board, and he continued writing when he could.

The next phase of Father's life, then, came when he published *Laughing Boy*, in 1929. The book is a novel about the life of a Navajo youth, Laughing Boy, and his bride, Slim Girl. Building on his anthropological background, the story became and remains enormously popular. The book is magical because it is a look into the romantic exotic—the life of an unassimilated Indian—a life which was unknown to almost everyone, as seen through that which is common to everyone, a love story. Indeed, the book was so highly regarded, so unusual, so tactile in its descriptions that it won the Pulitzer Prize for 1930.

The substantial success of the book, followed by the O. Henry Prize in 1931 for "Haunted Ground," gave father the high profile to sell everything he wrote, both short stories and novels. In part, his success came from his approach to writing about American Indians, an approach that eschewed the more popular sentimental and mannered view of their lives, in favor of a style both realistic and anthropologically accurate. For a portion of the thirties, Father rode upon that success, having, as his brother, Francis, recalled, black-tie dinners every night, and living the high life. Eventually, however, he became wearied by his success and the shallowness of his life and by having to write upon Indians whether he wanted to or not. At some point, he decided there were too many other topics on which he wanted to write, too many other stories, so he made the brave and deliberate decision to stop writing about Indians, to stop his effortless success, to become a writer who depended upon his work, not upon his fame.

As Father later recalled, this ended the gravy-train. Although he remained a highly respected author and was widely read for the rest of his life, he never again achieved the success or comfort of what one might call his "Laughing Boy period."

The change brought both good and ill. For good, he was freed to write as he wanted, to conduct his life out of the public eye, to live free of the expectations of the famous, of his class, of the east coast. However, he later said with some bitterness, he was continually asked, "Have you ever written anything else?"

Also for ill, Father divorced his first wife, Wanden Matthews, and, thereby, lost considerable contact with his first two children, Povy, and Pete.

Father continued his work in all three fields—Indian rights, anthropology, and creative fiction. Gradually, his work on anthropology lessened as the other two fields demanded more time and effort and generated more rewards, that is, a living.

In New York, in 1939, Father married my mother, who had gone to the city to find her fame and fortune. Of the six children in her family, Mother was the only one not to go to college, not because of inability but because of lack of interest. Mother was a self-described "party girl," more interested in having fun than in academics—she did well in both, but was especially able in the former. New York City promised unrealized horizons, and Consuelo Baca soon found success as a beauty and as a hat-check girl at Jack and Charlie's 21 Club. Father became fascinated by the Spanish exotic with a brain and a love of books, proposed, and they were married. Soon thereafter, they returned to their best-beloved area, New Mexico, and lived in Tesuque Village, just north of Santa Fe.

The next detour in Father's career came with World War II. As a self-described "Anglomaniac" during the Great War, he had wanted to fight for "dear old England." He had been, however, too young, at sixteen and seventeen years of age. Frustrated at not having been able to contribute, Father was determined to enter the lists when America entered the Second World War. As his health had become somewhat precarious, and as he was no longer a youth (he was 39 in 1942), he failed the physical to enter the armed forces. He was not to be stopped. Father then went to Mother's gynecologist and was passed. He entered the Officers' Training Corps, then served in Washington—where Mother spent the War working as a secretary—and overseas in the China-Burma-India Theater as the official historian of the Armed Transport Command. From this came an unusual book about the birth of that organization of the armed forces, *The Eagle in the Egg*.

After the War ended, the two returned to Santa Fe, where they bought the house I yet live in, and where I was born.

It is worth taking a moment to consider why Mother and Father wanted to live in Santa Fe.

First, of course, New Mexico had been the home of my mother's family, the Bacas, for centuries. Mother loved her home state, and, also, missed her family. Second, Father loved New Mexico, the home of the exotic cultures of the Spanish and of the numerous Indian tribes. Third, because of the last, there was no place better for Father to conduct his business of Indian rights work, for here there were not only many tribes but, also, many Whites both knowledgeable and interested and committed. Last, and least obvious, Santa Fe had been an artists' colony since the early twentieth century. This made for a conducive environment for Father's work as a writer and, also, as a person.

Santa Fe had begun to attract artists in some number in the 1920's, after the Great War ended. What the artists found was what had been discovered by the anthropologists and trappers before them in the nineteenth century, a frontier state which not only afforded them physical room and freedom but, also, a population that was open-minded and had a live-and-let-live attitude. For those who did not fit in elsewhere, Northern New Mexico, in general, and Taos and Santa Fe, in particular, offered freedom from restriction, from convention, and from expectations of either family or society.

Santa Fe had attracted a society of painters, sculptors, writers, poets, eccentrics, and patrons of the arts who appreciated the opportunity and the honor of being in the presence of creative talent. Many of these same patrons were also the same people who were interested in saving, and conserving, and encouraging the Indian and Spanish cultures, both of which were struggling to find their places in the twentieth century, even to survive.

Now, it may not seem particularly exemplary that Santa Fe offered a place to "be one's self" in today's culture. Today, one is encouraged to be "true to one's self," to be an individual, to be a rebel, to consider one's self unique and important on a regular basis. One must remember, however, that up until the Baby Boom turned the nation upside down in the sixties, for good and for ill, that these attitudes were much muted and that society emphasized one's duty to family and to society. The pressure to fit in and to conform was, at times, overwhelming. Small-town culture, with its suffocating atmosphere of convention and conformity, was yet the Culture of the United States. This is not to say that this was all wrong or bad, merely that it was so. There was, however, a place where one could escape these influences of convention and conformity, and it, too, was a small town—Santa Fe.

I don't wish to paint Father as a wild-eyed bohemian. I have known wild eyed, and I have known bohemian, and he was not either. Nor do I wish to paint Santa Fe as being full of either radicals or of great writers and artists, but there were both, enough of each to be intriguing, rewarding, and revivifying for someone who wanted to "escape."

In any case, what anyone of even minor curiosity would find was a culture of creativity and of imagination in which being one's self, for good or ill, was encouraged. Such an atmosphere was rewarding for patrons of the arts, as well, whether they patronized Anglo poets or wished to save the Indian or Spanish cultures. They often ran parties and dinner-tables at which the widest possible range of people were thrown together. In fact, Mother often stressed to me that a good party, a good Santa Fe party was one in which the gamut ran from elegant aristocrats to youths to dirt-poor artists to Indians. Her mother had taught her this after the family's move from the ranch at Rociada to Santa Fe, when Grandmother became Secretary of State in 1931. Grandmother had occasional "salons" at which all sorts were thrown together, especially with her young daughters and their friends. It was a primary principle of both my maternal grandparents that young people should be encouraged to listen to their elders, to learn, and to widen their horizons. This tradition was remarkably akin to the La Farge tradition, if rather less uproarious and argumentative. Then, because anyone who was anyone was introduced to my grandmother, her children were introduced to a wide range of people, indeed.

Further, Mother said, what mattered was not background, wealth, profession, ethnicity, creed, or other distinction. What mattered was what one brought to the table. If one was interesting and had something to say, one was welcome and others were welcoming. If one had nothing to contribute, status and wealth mattered not, that person was discarded.

For a writer, then, from a family famed not for its business acumen, its wealth, its power, or its influence, but, rather, for its creativity in all fields of thought and artistic endeavor, Santa Fe was a natural fit.

I could tell, from what he said, that father felt completely comfortable here—at home, in the truest sense of the term, natural and comfortable. He cared deeply about the town and threw himself into working for its benefit, not merely as a civic duty—another family tradition—but because he felt it vitally important that the City Different be kept from being ruined by commercial, development, or merely ignorant interests.

Father could always find his way back to his roots, when he wanted, and he went east each and every year for the annual meeting of the Indian association, where he stayed at the Century Club, in New York City. This was a journey he loved, if only because he could eat sea-food, but also, because of family, and childhood setting, and a return to beginnings. This journey also reminded him of what he valued here and why he wished to return. Here he might not, as he did when a youth, dance at the Vanderbilts' under dripping candles, to go home in his tails with candle-wax on his shoulders, but he could relax completely into interesting, intellectual, and creative society, one with more to offer than insistence on convention as a beginning point.

One might say Father began one last career in Santa Fe, that was, keeping watch on Santa Fe. During the fifties, he threw himself into the work of historic preservation, preservation of both individual buildings and of the town itself, to the point that, with no prior training, he and a small group, including architect John Gaw Meem, Samuel Montoya, and urban planner Irene von Horvath, created Santa Fe's original Historic District Ordinance to preserve the look, feel, and authenticity of the oldest part of the city.

It is true, even then, even before our day, that the city and its claim to authenticity were under attack; thereby, it was considered the province of all good men to spring to her defense lest that sooner rather than later there would be nothing left to defend. As Father wrote during the battle for the doomed Nusbaum Building, "We can require that new buildings comply with certain style requirements. Fine. But pull out all the really old ones, everything that really backs up the city's claim to age, authenticity, and a special culture, and pretty soon it will look like a mouthful of false teeth, with a single old molar, the Governors' Palace, in one corner. Nobody, but nobody, will cross the continent just to look at a well-constructed set of dentures."

One may hear, here, his passion and his love for his adopted town, a town where he could live as he was most comfortable, in the midst of that which was being rapidly lost elsewhere, that which he had sought all over the southwest, all over North America, and had protected in the guise of the Indians, that which he had tried to tease apart in Mesoamerica—cultural integrity.

In his autobiography, *Raw Material*, Father wrote a superior account of one man's life. As Mother pointed out, it was superior because it was not a mere accounting of what, when, how, and in what order, rather, it was the account of how the raw material of one boy grew into a man, a man whose life both displayed and sought out true integrity.

John Pen La Farge. *Photograph courtesy of John Pen La Farge Archives*

IV

OLIVER LA FARGE
(1901–1963)
by
Edith Bayles Ricketson

El Palacio magazine, Summer 1964 issue.

Although Oliver La Farge was born in New York, spent most of his early years there and in Rhode Island, and was educated at Eastern institutions (Groton School, Harvard University, B.A. cum laude, 1924; M.A. in Anthropology, 1929), during the last two-thirds of his life he was strongly attached, intellectually and emotionally, to the American Southwest and the peoples and cultures of New Mexico and Arizona. His first acquaintance with the Navajo and Hopi Indians was made on Peabody Museum archaeological expeditions to Arizona, in 1921 and 1922 as a student worker, and in 1924 as director. Subsequent pack trips, some quite extended, in the Indian country of the Southwest, developed his knowledge of and interest in Indian people and their problems; and these experiences not only provided much material for his popular writing, but also shaped the expertise which he later put to such excellent use as a director and president of the Eastern Association on Indian Affairs from its organization, with time out for the war years, until his death.

During these "early years," roughly 1925 to 1940, he was also occupied with academic studies, which included research and teaching at Harvard, Tulane, Columbia, the University of Pennsylvania and field work in Mexico and Guatemala, which resulted in four substantial technical reports and numerous articles on ethnology and linguistics, chiefly of Highland Maya Indian groups. He was also writing fiction and, after the success of his first novel, *Laughing Boy* (Pulitzer Prize, 1930), he considered writing his profession and anthropology his avocation. His novels and short stories dealing with Indians and their problems are pre-eminent in their ability to give the average reader an understanding of what it is like to be an Indian.

In 1941 he returned to New Mexico to establish permanent residence in Santa Fe, where he had lived briefly in the mid-1930s, but in 1942 he was called to Washington to become historian of the AAF Air Transport Command. He was commissioned captain in 1943, separated as lieutenant colonel in 1946, and received the Legion of Merit. His military service completed, Santa Fe was thenceforward to be his home, and he joined enthusiastically in community efforts to preserve its historic and cultural distinction. He served as one of the founding Board Members of the Museum of Navajo Ceremonial Art and was its Vice-President until 1958 when he became President. He was a member of the Advisory Council of The Old Santa Fe Association from 1948 until his death; and in 1956-1957 he served on the City Planning Commission. From 1953 until 1963 he wrote a lively and literate weekly column called "The Santa Fe Bird Watcher" for the local newspaper, *The Santa Fe New Mexican.*

Other honors accorded Oliver La Farge in his lifetime, not mentioned above, include the following: Fellow, American Anthropological Association; Fellow, American Association for the Advancement of Science; Member, National Institute of Arts and Letters; Member, American Academy of Arts and Sciences; Member, White House Advisory Committee; Honorary M.A., Brown University, 1932.

But the achievement for which Oliver La Farge will be long remembered, and certainly most widely, was in the field of Indian affairs. His concern for the problems of American Indians was genuine, personal as well as academic, and his zeal in their behalf, untiring. Newspaper tributes at the time of his death generally acclaimed him "one of the greatest champions of the rights of the American Indians"; tributes and expressions of sorrow from tribal officials and other Indian friends all over the United States poured in to his family and to the Association on American Indian Affairs, which he represented so vigorously. Expressions of respect and friendship came also from U.S. Government officials, with whom he often battled but with whom he also worked gladly and generously when he felt his aims and theirs were jointly for the betterment of Indian life, health and economy. In 1936 his particular task for the Bureau of Indian Affairs was the drafting of a constitution for the Hopi tribe, which was later adopted. He helped prepare an alphabet for writing the Navajo language, with the use of which members of the tribe were able to publish a Navajo newspaper. He was frequently called by tribal attorneys to testify as a technical assistant before hearings of the Indian Claims Commission. His unquestioned background knowledge of historical and actual conditions and his gift for precise expression made his frequent speaking appearances at Congressional hearings and other meetings truly memorable. The breadth and depth of his influence and active participation in nationwide Indian and Santa Fe community affairs has yet to be fully realized.

Considering his notable accomplishments in the diverse fields of science, arts, belles letters, history and humanitarianism, Oliver La Farge appears to have been truly a 20th Century "Renaissance man" . . . but anyone who ventured to make that suggestion in his presence would have been nicked very neatly by the rapier-like wit which he knew how to wield so deftly.

V

COCHISE OF ARIZONA

COCHISE
of Arizona

COCHISE
of Arizona

by OLIVER La FARGE

Illustrated by L. F. BJORKLUND

PREFACE

This story is fiction based on fact. The characters of Cochise, Ward, Bascom, Jeffords, Mangas Coloradas, and General Howard are historical, as are a few of the minor characters. I have described them as the histories make them seem. The main incidents are also true. These are the kidnapping of Mickey Free, Bascom's treachery and the beginning of the Chiricahua War, the Battle of Apache Pass, the Arivaipa and Pinaleño massacres, and the murder of Mangas Coloradas. The story of Jefford's friendship with Cochise is true, and so is the way in which General Howard made peace.

Most of the conversations are invented. So are the minor incidents and the description of the raid into Mexico. To the best of my ability, I have tried to make these true to life, even though they are fiction.

Preface

Some of the names in this story cause people trouble. It does not matter much if many of them are pronounced incorrectly. There are some that readers should get right, however. Cochise is pronounced Ko-CHEESS. Chiricahua is pronounced Chi-ri-KAH-wa. Tucson, now a thriving American city, is always pronounced Too-SAHN. Heaven knows what that "c" is doing in there.

Most of the accounts say that Cochise called Jeffords "younger brother." I think that this is an error. When he was old, Jeffords said that Cochise called him by an Apache term which the man listening to him wrote down as "Chickasaw." No such word exists in Apache. The word for younger brother does not sound like that at all. The nearest thing to it is *"shikis"* which means "my sister's son." That is a close, strong relationship among the Apaches, much stronger than with us. Therefore, in this story, Cochise calls Jeffords "nephew."

For the history I have depended especially upon Frank Lockwood's *The Apaches*. I have known a few Chiricahuas slightly, but I have never lived among them as I have among some of the other Apaches. Therefore I have made much use of Morris Opler's *An Apache Lifeway*, which is the best of all scientific descriptions of the Chiricahuas.

O. La F.

# CHAPTER I

⛭ UP IN THE MOUNTAINS WHERE the Chiricahua Apaches lived, October mornings were crisply cold. Cochise, chief of the Chiricahuas, pulled his blanket about him and lifted his face to the sun. He was well over six feet tall, well made, strong. He was nearly fifty years old, but he moved like an athlete. In the Apache style, his long hair fell to his shoulders on either side of his face. Around his head a piece of blue cloth was bound.

His face was strong and stern. Many who knew him have described him as handsome, in an Indian way, with a high nose, wide cheekbones, and a firm mouth. Now, the sternness of his expression was specially noticeable. He was frowning slightly. As he stood in front of his hut, taking the sun on his forehead, he was thinking of omens, bad omens.

Last night he had dreamed of White-Eyes. He had seen many White-Eye soldiers dressed in their blue uniforms, carrying their rifles. They had forgotten that there was peace between the White-Eyes and the Chiricahuas. He woke up before the dream went any further. Nothing had happened; there had simply been that bad dream.

Then, as he reached for the basket of broiled deer meat his wife had prepared for breakfast, for a moment his right hand had trembled. He thought that that was certainly an omen, a sign of something happening far away.

He decided that later on he would go talk to a medicine man, to find out what these things might mean. At the moment, as he looked about him, everything spoke of peace in the land.

The Chiricahua houses were dome-shaped. They were covered with a thatch of dried grass. Over this, deerskins or blankets were often laid, as added protection against rain and cold. At the very top of the dome there was a hole. The fire was directly under this. Cochise could see half a dozen houses from where he stood. The smoke rose up in grey, thin columns from most of them. Further away he could see smoke from others, hidden by the pine trees or by folds of the mountains.

The Chiricahuas did not build their houses too close together. Families liked to be alone. Also, the tribe kept itself always ready for war, even in a time of peace.

If the whole village were huddled together, an enemy making a surprise attack could get all through it before the alarm was given. With their homes scattered, hidden away, only a few could be surprised. The warriors would have time to seize their weapons. They could assemble before an enemy could get to most of them.

The settlement was arranged against the danger of attack, but the place spoke of peace. The very fact that every family had a well-made house was a sign of peace. In times of serious war, when the whole tribe might have to move at a moment's notice, they lived in the simplest kind of shelters. They could pack up and be on the move in little more than five minutes. What they left behind for an enemy to find was hardly worth burning.

No one was in such shelters now. At a distance, Cochise heard a man singing a pleasure song. In front of one house, two women were laughing as they watched a baby pulling at the reeds of an unfinished basket. The increasing warmth of the sun mixed with the crisp air. It was good to be alive on such a morning.

There was no cause for worry, Cochise thought. He had made peace with the White-Eyes five years ago, and they were glad of it. Ever since, their stagecoaches and wagons had passed freely through Apache Pass, a few miles away. Mail and supplies were carried between their city of Tucson, west of the Chiricahuas, and that mysterious eastern country from which the White-Eyes had come.

Cochise did more than let the traffic pass through his country, he protected it from the other Apache tribes. Half a dozen Chiricahua families had built houses near the Overland Mail Station, making a business of providing it with firewood and wild hay. There were no soldiers at the Station, only four peaceful White-Eyes. A couple of these had learned to speak Apache fairly well. His people traded with them. All the signs pointed towards peace.

Of course, Cochise thought, you could never entirely trust those people. They did very strange things. So you worried about their presence in the land. You worried about how there were so many of them, so many of their soldiers, when your people were few. As a result of that, you could give yourself dreams about them. He would see the medicine man, he would have himself cured of the dream, but he did not need to worry too much.

The chief had already made his morning prayer, but now as his spirit relaxed, in his thoughts he prayed again, briefly. He asked White Painted Woman and Child of the Waters for peace, goodheartedness, and right thinking in all the land.

The chief heard men's voices calling instructions and encouragement a slight distance away. After listening a moment, he knew what was going on. Smiling slightly, he moved in that direction to watch.

Eight young athletes who were about to turn into men, boys sixteen years old, were lined up in two rows along either side of a small valley. The place was little more than a long, shallow, grassy depression. The two lines of four boys were about a hundred feet apart. To their right and left stood several older men, coaching them. Cochise stood among the trees, looking down.

The warriors-about-to-be were stripped to breechclouts and moccasins. They carried bows in their left hands, and each had a number of arrows stuck in the ground in front of him.

The arrows had dull, wooden ends. The bows were made by the boys themselves under instruction of the men who were training them and they were fairly strong. If anyone should be hit by one of those arrows, shot at that distance, he was not likely to be killed or seriously injured, but he would get a wound to remember.

They were playing a game, the purpose of which was to teach them to shoot quickly and carefully, and to dodge arrows. First, the boys on one side would fire several rounds at the others, then the second side would take a turn.

As Cochise stood watching, it was the turn of the boys on the north side. They shot rapidly. It took a quick eye to follow the flight of the arrows, but the four opposite them dodged them all. Two of the receivers suc-

ceeded in knocking shafts aside with their hands.

It was by training such as this that the Chiricahuas made themselves into great warriors. At the time that boys were turning into men, they went through many tests. They learned to run for miles through the hottest, sandiest desert, to lie for long periods of time without moving. They learned to endure heat, cold, hunger, and thirst. They would take a mouthful of water, then run two miles in the hot sun. When they finished, they would spit out the water to show that they had not swallowed it.

The Chiricahuas were a small tribe. When all their warriors were gathered together, there were less than three hundred of them. Yet no one wanted to have trouble with them. Even the White-Eye soldiers were glad to be at peace with them. There were many more soldiers than there were Chiricahua warriors, and they had much better weapons. But no one could fight like a Chiricahua.

Now the boys on the north made ready to dodge. Cochise heard a step. His nephew, Mesquite, came to stand alongside him. Mesquite had become a man this spring, and was now a novice warrior. A novice had to go with four war parties, not to fight, but to serve the men. Then he, too, became a grown man and a warrior. Mesquite had gone as a servant three times, and had one more time to go. The chief acknowledged his nephew's presence, then both turned to watch the game.

The shooter on the east end of the south row played a clever trick. As he nocked his first arrow, he took a second in his left hand, holding it so that it lay along the outer side of the bow. The receiver facing him did not seem to notice it.

The shooter sent an arrow slightly to the left, so that if the receiver had not dodged, it would have struck his left shoulder. He had not drawn the bowstring back to the full; the arrow traveled a little slower than usual, in a higher arc, easier to see. The boy opposite moved his body to the right, and triumphantly, with a faint smile, caught the arrow out of the air with his left hand.

That was just what the shooter had planned on. He waited until the boy's attention was set on the approaching arrow, and his body, twisted to the right, was off balance. Then he nocked and shot the second arrow. His hands moved like lightning. The draw was to full length, the arrow flew straight and fast.

It struck the receiver's right shoulder before he even knew it was coming.

Cochise and Mesquite could hear the smack as the arrow struck. The boy gave a start of pain. His lips parted, but he did not cry out. He set his face into calmness, pulled the arrow from his bleeding shoulder, and called out, "You are generous with your arrows this morning!" There was laughter. The older warriors in charge of the training gave praise, and pointed out where the injured boy had done wrong.

Cochise told his nephew, "That was fine shooting. And that boy there—he has courage. He will be more alert from now on. I think we shall have two more good warriors."

"What will there be for them to do?" Mesquite asked. It was as far as he dared go in reproaching his uncle for the state of peace in which the Chiricahuas lived.

For a moment Cochise's expression moved towards anger, then it relaxed. He looked at the young man, proudly and fondly. Here, he knew, was a fine warrior, a warrior worthy of Cochise's line. This young man had been ready to complete his service as a novice since the time of Little Eagles. In the nearly six months since then, there had been only three war parties for him to go with.

"I know, nephew," Cochise said. "I served my four war parties all within two moons. It is slow for you, but do not worry. We may yet see war until even we, the Chiricahua People, are sick of it. Your war parties will come."

"Why must we let the White-Eyes go and come through our country?"

"Do you not like the trade goods? That shirt you are wearing, does it not please you?"

"I like these things, but I like even better what I take for myself, like a man. And I like buckskin and deer hide," Mesquite said.

His uncle nodded understandingly. Then he said, "There are many reasons for being at peace with the White-Eyes, which you have heard as you listened to the leaders talking. And there is one reason—I have given my promise." When Cochise said "I" he used a special word which means that a chief is speaking not for himself alone, but for his people.

The young man did not answer. He went back to watching the game. There was no good in further talking. Everyone knew that

Cochise's word was sacred. He never told a lie; he never broke a promise. He had no mercy for anyone who did. Any suggestion that he should lie or go against his word might cost the life of the one who made it.

Cochise turned away. He felt happy to see those young, strong boys who would soon be added to the number of his warriors. He believed that the only way that one can have peace is to be strong. The White-Eyes were very strong. There seemed to be no end to their numbers. They wanted the whole earth. If the Chiricahuas were to keep their little piece of the earth, this land which was their home and which they loved with all their hearts, they needed all their strength.

He shook his head slightly, as if to rid it of heavy thoughts. It was a worrying thing to be chief. A chief had to think of all the things that might hurt his people, he had to be always watching.

He walked towards a group of houses near a sunny, golden cliff. The medicine man lived in the nearest one. He would go to him and be cured of his dream. After that, he thought, he would talk to his brother, Thin Man, whom he loved.

CHAPTER II

ON THIS SAME OCTOBER MORN-
ing, west of the Chiricahua's territory, in the
Sonoita Valley, a six-year-old boy was playing. Out on the sandy flat beyond the corral of
the ranch where he lived, he was pretending
to lasso a donkey. The donkey was browsing
about, looking for anything it could find to
eat. It moved slowly from one straggly bush
to another, examining them for green leaves.
It paid little attention to the boy.

Six men were watching the boy from
hiding. The men were lying behind a low,
sandy ridge. They wore breechclouts, mocca-

sins that came up to their knees like boots, and headbands. That was all. Their long, black hair hung loose down their backs. There was red and black paint on their faces. Two of them carried old flintlock guns. The other four had bows and arrows. All of them had knives.

These men belonged to a tribe known as Pinal Apaches, or Pinaleños, because they lived near a place called Pinal, a hundred miles or so to the north. In those days there were many different tribes of Apaches, living in Arizona, in New Mexico, and in Mexico. The pale-skinned men from the east had come and had said that this part of the Apache country belonged to them. They said another part of it, further south, belonged to Mexico.

The Apaches did not think that anyone, Mexicans or White-Eyes, had a right to divide their country, or to claim ownership of it. They refused to admit that anyone but themselves owned their country. They called the pale men "White-Eyes," because they thought that their gray eyes really had no color.

For a great many years all the Apache tribes had been at war with Mexico. They had started this war because the Mexicans once had tried to rule all their country, so they decided to drive the Mexicans out. The war had gone on and on.

Later, when the White-Eyes claimed the right to rule part of their land, they had started fighting them. At the time when those six men lay watching the little boy at play, which was in October of the year 1860, all but one of the Apache tribes was at war against the White-Eyes.

There was war all up and down the land, over all the southern part of Arizona and New Mexico. The great chief known as Mangas Coloradas, or Red Sleeves, had united all the Apache tribes except one. That one was the Chiricahua Apaches, who lived in the mountains east of the Sonoita Valley. Their Chief, Cochise, had made peace. Although he was a friend of Mangas Coloradas, and admired him greatly, he had refused to join in the war.

These six Pinal Apaches were making a raid close to the Chiricahua territory. They did not go into that territory, because if they had, the Chiricahuas would have fought them. They had come to this ranch, although it was only twelve miles from Fort Buchanan, where there were many White-Eye soldiers. They had done this, because they had a special interest in this little boy.

They were not afraid of the soldiers. Apaches could sneak right up to the fort itself, and the soldiers would never catch them. If a Pinaleño so much as set foot in the land of the Chiricahuas, the Chiricahuas would know about it right away. But he could go and come as he pleased in the country the soldiers guarded.

The little boy's name was Miguel. His mother was a Mexican woman whom a Pinal Apache had captured years before. The Apache had married her, and was the father of her child. When Miguel was still very small, his mother had run away from the Pinaleños. Now, she was keeping house for a rancher named John Ward.

Ward had become fond of Miguel, and had adopted him. He considered him his son, but the Pinaleños considered that he belonged to them.

The leader of the war party was one of the men who had a musket. From his hiding place, his ambush, he looked around carefully in all directions. He saw no one except his own men and the little boy. Just after sunrise, he had watched John Ward get on a horse and ride away. There was no sign yet of his returning. He knew that Miguel's mother was somewhere inside the ranch house.

In the corral he could see a dozen horses and several oxen. The time had come, the Apache decided, to take the boy back, and to get some booty besides. He raised his hand to catch the attention of his followers, then he made a scooping motion.

As Miguel played, he drew nearer to the Pinaleños. They lay motionless; they seemed to sink into the earth. When he was only a few steps from them, the leader gave a call, and the men sprang up. Miguel screamed, turned to run, and fell. A warrior picked him up, and the Indians ran for the corral.

Miguel's mother came to the door and stood there, screaming. She did not dare try to take her son back; she knew that if she tried to interfere, the Indians would kill her. The Pinaleños paid no attention to her. They were busy with the horses.

They did not need saddles or bridles. Like all Apaches, they were expert horsemen. A piece of rope or a buckskin thong tied around a horse's jaw was enough for them. In no time at all six of the Apaches were mounted, one still holding the boy. They herded the other horses and the oxen out of the corral and were off, riding as fast as the heavy oxen could be made to go. Miguel's mother stood in the doorway, screaming and weeping, until they were out of sight.

It was in the afternoon before John Ward returned to his ranch. He was a big, strong man, brave, and warmhearted. He was also hot-tempered and extremely stubborn. He made enemies easily, and he never forgave them. He found his housekeeper sitting in his armchair, worn out from weeping. She could hardly speak, but she managed to tell him what had happened.

Immediately, he got back on his horse. He had a pistol on his hip and a rifle fastened to his saddle. Though he was alone, he set out at once to trail the Apaches. The trail led steadily to the east. He followed it until he reached the San Pedro River. By then it was getting dark. A short distance beyond the river began the country of the Chiricahuas, which no one dared enter without permission. He saw that his chase was hopeless, so he turned back.

As he rode home, he cursed the Chiricahuas and their chief, Cochise. Like many white men, he did not believe that any Indian would

keep a promise. He did not believe the Chiricahuas were at peace with the United States; he thought that that was just a lie.

The tracks of the stolen animals led eastward. The Chiricahuas lived to the eastward. So, he was sure that the Chiricahuas had made that raid. He was determined to have revenge, and he was ready to move heaven and earth to get the boy back.

CHAPTER III

COLONEL PITCAIRN MORRISON sat behind his desk in his adobe-walled office at Fort Buchanan. The morning sun came in through two smallish, high windows. Its light glinted on his brass buttons and the insignia on his shoulders. The room was pleasantly cool, although a little too dark for an office. Later in the day it would be stuffy, although the walls were thick and adobe does not let much heat pass.

Colonel Morrison commanded the Seventh Infantry Regiment, stationed here at Fort Buchanan, and he was in charge of the other, smaller bodies of troops stationed in southern Arizona and New Mexico. He had a difficult job, and he was not happy with it.

For one thing, his wife did not like it at Fort Buchanan. There were no cities nearby. The nearest town of any size at all was Tucson, and to get there was a long, hard drive. In good weather the roads were dusty, in bad weather they were muddy. In any kind of weather they were rough. In any kind of weather, too, there might be Apaches along the road, and Apaches had no more respect for a colonel's wife than for anybody else.

If she wanted to visit Tuscon, she had to have an escort of troops. When she got to Tuscon, she had not reached much of any-where. It was a shabby little town, full of rough people. Many of the inhabitants spoke only Spanish. There was very little amuse-ment for officer's wives, or even for officers, to find there.

Mrs. Colonel Morrison often spoke to her husband about getting transferred. She wanted him moved to some other place, to somewhere more civilized. The colonel would have liked a transfer himself. So would many of his officers and men. Life at Fort Buchanan was dull and often hard. Worse than that, it gave one a feeling of uselessness.

Colonel Morrison commanded a regiment of United States Infantry. What he needed was cavalry. His job was to protect miles and miles of country against the Apaches, and there were times when he could hardly protect the fort. The Apaches did not come out and fight regular battles. If they had, he thought he could have whipped them. He had as many men as they, and much better weapons. Apaches raided. They ran away. They hid. Very often, when his men pursued them, the Indians ambushed them. It made his men feel helpless and ashamed.

Fort Buchanan was not really a fort. It was a number of buildings placed around a parade ground, but no walls enclosed it. From time to time Apaches raided the fort itself. Sometimes a little party of only five or six of them would make a raid against a whole regiment; sometimes there would be more.

For an officer, proud of the American Army, proud of his regiment, these raids were most humiliating. There would be a sound in the night, some shots, some wild yelling. Before the troops could turn out and grapple with the enemy, the enemy would be far away.

Perhaps a sentry or two would have been killed. Horses might be run off, or cattle that had been bought to feed the regiment might be stolen. Sometimes a building would be set on fire. The Apaches almost always got some equipment, if only the rifle and ammunition of a sentry they had killed.

All the way round, Colonel Morrison thought, he did not like this post. A few weeks ago, the Apaches had stolen his own best horse. There did not seem to be anything to do about it. He kept sending out the few mounted men he had to chase after one group or another, but he did not have nearly enough. He needed a regiment of cavalry. Perhaps he needed a brigade.

The country was very big. As like as not, in one day he would get news of trouble in three or four different places, hundreds of miles apart.

The colonel did not like to think that even the Overland Mail, the stagecoaches, and the supply wagons came from the East only because an Apache chief gave them permission. The straight route from the East ran through Apache Pass, in the Chiricahua country.

Major Steen, who had commanded here before he came, had made peace with the Chiricahuas. Steen told him that their chief, Cochise, was a man of honor. Morrison found that hard to believe. Who ever heard of an Indian being a man of honor?

True, for five years now the traffic had run through Apache Pass without any trouble at all. Perhaps it was a trick. Perhaps, he thought, Cochise let the wagons go through the Pass so as to seem friendly. Perhaps at the same time he raided the ranches, the villages, the mines, just like the others. Major Steen had said not. Steen knew Cochise personally. He respected him. Perhaps, the colonel thought, he should try to meet this famous man.

He had suggested this once in Tucson, and everyone argued against it. They told him that there was too much danger. Cochise, they said, was the most ruthless of all the Indian chiefs. The Tucson people, instead, wanted him to take all his troops and start a real war against the Chiricahuas. They wanted him to wipe out these savages.

Colonel Morrison knew very little about Indians. He was not even really good at fighting them, although he did his best. He thought the same things about them that many people did in those days. His ideas about Indians came from stories passed on from person to person, from place to place. Many of these stories had no truth in them at all.

Still, the colonel was not a fool. He knew why the Tucson people wanted him to attack the Chiricahuas. There were two reasons. When there was much fighting, they made more money supplying the troops. And then, the Chiricahua country was rich. There was good timber there. Tuscon settlers believed that there was gold in the area. They would like to see the Apaches driven out of it so that they could have it for themselves.

He thought of that talk. He had all the trouble he could handle right now. He was not going to start a war with the worst fighters of all, just to suit some selfish men in Tucson. He began thinking again of how he could arrange a meeting with Cochise.

His clerk-sergeant came in and saluted. "Mr. Ward is here to see the colonel. He says his business is urgent, sir."

The colonel sighed. Urgent business around here usually meant just one thing. "Show him in."

Ward entered the room. His clothes were dusty from twelve miles of steady riding. He brushed aside the colonel's greeting.

He said, "Colonel, those cursed savages raided my ranch yesterday. They ran off twelve of my horses and almost all my oxen." He paused a moment, then he said, heavily. "And, they kidnapped my little boy."

"The boy you adopted?"

"Yes." It was plain to see that John Ward was greatly upset.

"Oh! That's too bad!" said the colonel. "I'm truly sorry, Mr. Ward."

"What are you going to do about it?" snapped the rancher.

"This happened yesterday?"

"Yes," Ward replied impatiently.

Colonel Morrison drummed on his desk with his fingertips. "There is not much I can do. What mounted troops I have are all out already, and it would be useless to try to chase them with infantry."

Ward snorted. "Go to their ranchería and take him back. And while you're at it, kill a few of the devils."

"Mr. Ward, you have my utmost sympathy, but I cannot comb every Apache ranchería in the Territory. You know that."

"Just one ranchería, Colonel."

The colonel raised his eyebrows. "Which one?"

"The Chiricahuas'. Where that murderin' Cochise lives."

Colonel Morrison considered a moment. "The Chiricahuas? We have peace with the Chiricahuas."

"There isn't any peace with any Injuns

until you've killed the last of them. Sure, they let the wagons through the Pass. That keeps you happy." As he made this last statement, Ward sneered reproachfully. "In between times, they raid like all the rest of them."

"What makes you think these were Chiricahuas?" the colonel asked.

"I trailed them," Ward snapped. "They lit out due east. I followed the tracks clear to the San Pedro River. I turned back there because it was dark. They went on across. What's on the east of the San Pedro? Chiricahua country. It was Chiricahuas."

"I see. You may be right," Morrison acknowledged.

"I am right. Take your regiment and smack 'em. Burn 'em out."

The colonel said, "I fear I cannot do that. It would mean leaving all the rest of this country unguarded. As soon as I have some cavalry, I'll send an expedition."

Ward snorted again. His face grew red. Before he could speak, the colonel said, "We shall do everything we can, Mr. Ward. The first suitable troops I have will be sent after your boy. That is all I can do. Good day."

Ward stared at the officer a moment, then

turned on his heel and walked out without answering.

Both men were angry. The rancher was angry that the whole regiment was not turned out at once. It seemed to him that the soldiers were useless. He thought that the colonel was simply too lazy or too cowardly to go to the rescue. Colonel Morrison was angry in part because he was unable to act immediately on Ward's demand. Also, the rancher's humiliating manner annoyed him. He was accustomed to respect.

He got up and crossed the room to study the map on the wall. Ward was probably right; it looked as if Chiricahuas had stolen the boy.

But the Chiricahua country began some distance beyond the San Pedro River. Colonel Morrison realized that there was some room for doubt. Had he known that Miguel's own father belonged to the Pinaleños tribe, he would have been more doubtful still. Certainly he was not going to start a war that would close the Pass unless he was sure that the Chiricahuas were already on the warpath. When he could, he would send a mounted detail and try to get the boy back by negotiations.

He thought over possible difficulties. If he marched against Cochise's settlement, his ranchería, the Chiricahuas would most likely not be there when he reached it. There would be nothing but an endless running fight as the troops marched, a fight with an enemy they seldom saw. He did not have enough men to surround the place, even if he could do so before the Indians got away.

He was a military man. He faced the fact quite frankly that all the troops he had were too few to conquer the less than three hundred Chiricahua fighting men.

The one thing that Colonel Morrison did not think of was that he could arrange a peaceful meeting with Cochise. It did not occur to him that if the two of them talked as chief to chief, he could find out the truth.

The course of history is a strange thing. Events seem to follow upon each other like a river that must flow in its channel. And yet, from time to time, one can see how an accident, a chance, can control or shift its course. If mounted troops had been on hand that day, Colonel Morrison would have ordered them to follow up the raiders.

So many animals traveling in a bunch leave a fairly easy trail to follow. The troops would have crossed the San Pedro. They would have seen how the tracks turned north, and led away from the Chiricahuas. They might never have caught the raiders, they might never have known who stole the boy. They would, however, have known that it was done by men from one of the Apache tribes to the north. Pinaleños, Arivaipas, or White Mountain Apaches, not Cochise's people.

Colonel Morrison was angry with Ward. He did not want to be responsible for getting the Chiricahuas on the warpath. There was trouble north, south, east, and west. His troops were needed everywhere. Three months went by before he could arrange for an expedition of men to deal with Cochise.

As for little Miguel, it was many years before white men had news of him again. He grew up a Pinaleño, and later became well-known as an interpreter. As far as anyone knows, he was happy among his father's people, although he may have been frightened when they carried him off. When he was grown-up and dealt with white men, he went by the name of Mickey Free. His name remains in history because quite innocently he was the cause of great and terrible events.

CHAPTER IV

A LONE, YOUNG WARRIOR WALKED into the Chiricahua settlement. He passed by his own dwelling without stopping, and made his way directly to Cochise's. There he stood outside the door.

The chief looked up. Neither Cochise nor the young man spoke immediately; that would have been impolite. Good manners require that people allow each other a little time, to shift their minds from what they were thinking. They must have time to adjust themselves to another's presence. After some

39

seconds Cochise laid aside an arrow he was shaping and said, "Enter."

The man stooped under the top of the doorway and came in. Cochise made a gesture with one hand. The man sat down. Again there was a slight pause. Cochise knew that this warrior brought news of some importance. He had been sent with a small party to scout to the southward, along the Mexican border, and was back sooner than expected. That meant that something had happened that must be reported.

Cochise said, "You have news."

"Yes," said the scout. "Some of it is bad. Some Mexican soldiers came into our country. They crossed over the line that the White-Eyes say they have made in the earth. They are hunting scalps, and they have taken some."

"Who?" Cochise's face darkened.

"Red Bow, his wife, and one child," the warrior answered. "The wife was Tracker's daughter, the one who became a woman this summer. The child was her little brother."

The chief's lips set in a tight line. For a moment one could see in his face all the fierceness of which his enemies accused him.

"How was this?" he asked.

"The men went hunting, the women and children were gathering seeds. The men had looked around, they had seen no enemy that morning. Nothing moved. Then these soldiers rode up. They attacked the women. When that one and Tracker heard them scream, they came back."

The warrior could not avoid mentioning Red Bow's name the first time. Thereafter he spoke of him as "that one." The name would be heard once more, when Cochise announced his death; then it would never again be spoken.

"They had killed those two," the scout went on; "the other had run away. That one was careless, he showed himself while he was shooting at the Mexicans, and they shot him. Then Tracker was alone. There was nothing for him to do but turn back and look for his own wife. Then he made a smoke, and we went to him."

The scout paused again. Cochise's face was grave. He motioned to the man to continue.

"We trailed them. There are sixteen of them, all mounted. They had caught four horses, too. Fourteen of them have guns and two have lances. The chief man has a good uniform, the others are pretty

ragged. They were hunting around to see if they could find any of the ones who got away. I left Tracker and my two companions to watch them, and came here to tell you."

Cochise asked, "Where did this happen?"

The man described the place. Cochise got up and left his hut, the scout following. Out in the open, the chief lifted his voice, calling the men of the tribe. Without great effort he made his voice carry far. Quickly the men assembled, the warriors, armed and ready, and the old men, the counsellors.

Cochise gave them the news. There was a stir. Women had gathered behind the men. When they learned of the deaths, and the names of the dead had been spoken for the last time, several of them withdrew. They were close relatives. And now they must mourn. Cochise asked for counsel.

An old man spoke. The Mexicans must learn to keep their soldiers out of Chiricahua country. Those soldiers must be caught. It had been a long time since the Chiricahuas had made a raid; now was the time for it. Another said that winter was close at hand. Now was a good time to gather supplies. There was no need for debate; it was clear that every-one was thinking alike.

Cochise announced, "We must punish, and punish so that it will not be forgotten. If in so doing we capture horses, cattle, goods, slaves, so much the better. First, we must catch those soldiers. Get ready at once."

He sent a man to a high place, there to watch for signals from the scouts in the south. While the men were still bringing in their horses, this man sent up a smoke signal, passing on one that he had seen. The puffs of smoke said that the Mexicans were with-drawing.

Cochise took two hundred men, leaving only a small group to guard the ranchería. He did not expect any attack. If there should be one, the people would scatter until the war party could be brought back. They rode out in a long file, with scouts ahead and on the flanks. They moved rapidly, traveling as steadily as they could without wearing out their horses. For all the speed of their travel, they never ceased to be watchful. They saw and noted everything, every sign, every small animal that moved. They did this without effort; it was part of their training.

Five young men of sixteen, including Mesquite, went with the party as novices. They would not fight; their duty was to serve the warriors. When fighting started, they would be kept in safety. For Cochise's nephew and one of the others, this would be their fourth war party. They would be full warriors when they returned this time. On the next war party they would be in the front, in the places where danger was greatest.

At dusk they met Tracker. He showed them where the Mexicans had gone, heading back into their own country. They, too, were traveling fast, probably in fear of being pursued. The other two scouts were following them. Tracker did not go with the party. He had his dead to attend to.

The Chiricahuas pushed on. Sixteen

mounted men driving four extra horses, and moving in a hurry, were bound to leave a clear track. In addition, the two Apache scouts had left markers to show the way.

Cochise figured that he would catch up with the Mexicans some time the next day. They would travel fast and be on the watch until they were out of the southern Apache country, after that they would probably relax. He was not in a hurry; he simply wanted to be sure that they did not get away from him. In any case, he would go on into Mexico until he came to a settlement big enough to provide good plundering.

The war party rested only enough to keep the horses in condition. It moved quietly. Had someone been there to watch, he might first have seen the advance guards, slipping along to the right and the left. Then he would have heard the faint thud of unshod horses' feet, the unending, tireless jog trot.

There would have been no clink of spurs or of chains, none of the many noises made by the white man's cavalry. It would have seemed as if an army of shadows were passing, an army of dark ghosts. When they had gone by, a watcher might have wondered if they were real.

CHAPTER V

COCHISE HAD READ HIS ENEMIES' minds correctly. The troop of Mexicans, commanded by a Lieutenant Amadeo González, pushed on as fast as it could until it was clear out of Apache country. As they were at the end of their expedition, they were less careful than the Indians of the condition of their horses, with the result that they pretty well held their lead. At no time had they any idea that two Apaches were keeping watch.

In the middle of the next afternoon, hot and dusty, they came to a little settlement called San Felipe. The place was halfway between a village and a ranch. There were four small adobe houses in a line along the rutted trail that passed for a road. Behind the houses were corrals. At one side, below the spring, there was a small group of irrigated gardens.

It was a bleak little place, but it looked comfortable to Lieutenant González's troops. Here, they knew, they could get food and possibly a drink of mescal. They spurred their tired horses, and drew up before the houses.

The few people of the settlement made them welcome. González sold one of the captured horses. With money in his hands, he ordered the best meal the women could cook, and invited everyone to eat with him.

Life at San Felipe was dull except when the Indians made it dangerous. Everyone welcomed the celebration. The soldiers told stories of their raid, tales that had little or no relation to the facts. They displayed their scalps.

The Mexican government at that time was paying more than a hundred dollars each for scalps of Apache men, lesser sums for those of women and children. A couple of counties in the Territory of Arizona also offered such bounties. This practice led to a ruthless hunting of human beings. Since scalps cannot talk, it often happened that innocent, friendly Indians were shot down for profit.

The soldiers had scalps of a man, a woman, and a child. They had agreed, however, to claim two men and one child. After all, once the scalp has been taken, there is no way to tell whether its owner was a man or a woman. Children's scalps could usually be known by the finer and shorter hair. The soldiers had nearly four hundred dollars' (or eight hundred pesos') worth of human hair. They felt rich.

They ate, drank mescal, and boasted. No one noticed a smoke signal going up from a ridge a mile or so to the north. No one saw the young warriors creeping about under cover of the corrals, watching, counting people, listening.

Some of the men of the settlement went out to bring in their own horses. The watchful Apaches counted altogether thirty animals in the corrals. The men of San Felipe saw no one, but everything that happened at San Felipe that afternoon was known to Cochise. And he knew exactly how many men, women, and children were there.

When an Apache, above all a Chiricahua

Apache, makes war, he goes about it with all his being. Never does he relax his thoughts, and in his thoughts, he believes, there is great power. He gives as much thought to his creeping, his hiding, as to fighting.

From time to time, in the old days, Chiricahuas showed white friends how they hid, but the white men did not, and still do not, understand. The warriors could somehow disappear where one would have said that there was no cover at all.

At nightfall, the Mexicans posted two sentries, one at the east and one at the west end of the line of houses. They were not much worried about an attack; they were pretty sure by then that no one had followed them. The sentries took it easy. They were not watchful.

The Chiricahua scouts could go and come as they pleased in the night, they could cross the road, they could pass between the houses. They saw that the guard was changed near midnight, and they decided that it would be changed again shortly before dawn.

Cochise slept very little. The fight that was to come should not be a very hard one. All told, there were twenty-one men now in the settlement. True, a few men, well armed, behind the walls of an adobe house, could hold off a strong force if they were given a chance to set up their defense. But Cochise expected to surprise these people. He saw no reason why he should not succeed. If he did, then the fighting would be short and one-sided.

Still, all fighting is serious. He was the chief, he was responsible for everything that happened. Whoever among his people might be killed or wounded, he was responsible. Therefore, he must keep his thoughts steady, he must think over everything, he must be sure that he had overlooked nothing.

He must think, too, of White Painted Woman, the sacred goddess of the Chiricahuas, and her son, Child of the Waters. He must draw strength from them. Through them he must hope to receive strength and help from God, whom the Apaches called Yusn. Yusn is eternal, he is everywhere, all strength comes from him. Without his strength, there can be no success.

Cochise, as chief, tried to live in such a way that he would always be in harmony with Yusn. That was why he hated a lie. That was why he never broke a promise. That was why before any fight, no matter how easy it might seem, he let his thoughts rest on Yusn and asked for his help.

Also, as a good general, he attended to the practical things. He held half of his force in reserve, completely hidden from the settlement. He directed these men to wait there in case they should be needed, and to take care of the horses. The Chiricahuas had dismounted while their horses were still far from the settlement. They took this precaution for fear the horses in the corrals would smell them and call to them, as horses may do.

Cochise also sent scouts out along the road, to give warning in case anyone should come towards the settlement. Then he arranged the second half of his force, the half that he expected would be enough for the fight, around the houses, and gave them their instructions.

The guard was changed again before dawn, as the Chiricahuas expected. The new sentries were drowsy. Four skillful, young warriors crept near to each of them. The warriors lay close to the ground, the darkness of their bodies blending into the shadows and the darkness of bushes.

The two soldiers moved about from time

to time. One of them almost stepped on one of the Chiricahuas. The other sat down after a while, and lit a cigarette. There was a warrior a little more than three feet behind him. The Apache lay motionless, making no sound, moving not a muscle.

There was whiteness in the east. The darkness began to lighten. East of the settlement there was the sound of a fox bark; another bark answered from the west. South of it, by the corrals, a night bird's call was heard. There was the sound of another bird from the north. The sentries paid no attention to these voices, which told that everyone was in position and ready.

When a fox barked again, the warriors around the sentries rose to their feet. Their strong hands seized the men, wrenched away their guns, covered their mouths. Knives glimmered in the faint light. One sentry gave a single cry, the other never had a chance to make a sound.

From the four directions the Chiricahuas moved silently to the houses, while a few of them, following orders, went to the corrals to release the horses. At the door of each house stood a strong man carrying a heavy boulder.

All at the same moment, they smashed the boulders against the doors, breaking them open. With that the silence ended. Shouts, screams, and the thump and thud of men fighting came out of the houses.

There were a few shots. In a few minutes everything was quiet again. Three Apaches were wounded; none was killed. Three women and two children were taken prisoner. Also, at Cochise's orders, one of the soldiers was held as a prisoner. All the other men were dead.

The soldier was brought before Cochise. The chief spoke some Spanish, but he did not wish to talk to this man, whom he looked upon simply as a cowardly murderer. One of his men questioned him. The man was terrified. He hoped to save his life by telling everything the Indians wanted to know.

He told them that the Mexican soldiers belonged to the garrison at a village called Ocotal, two days' ride to the south. They said that there were about sixty men still there. He said that they were cavalry, and all of them were mounted, and that almost all had guns.

That was what Cochise wanted to know.

He gave a signal. One of his men stepped forward with a lance in his hand, and struck the soldier dead.

There was food in the houses. The Chiricahuas ate and rested. Then some of them rode out into the desert, rounding up what cattle and horses were browsing nearby. They made up a herd of nearly forty horses, including those belonging to the soldiers, and they gathered about twenty head of cattle.

Cochise had to decide what to do with the

prisoners. He thought nothing of killing all the men, but he did not like to kill women and children, although they were killed often enough in the deadly warfare of that time. Yet if he let them go, they might get to Ocotal and give warning. He decided to send them to his stronghold along with the extra horses and the cattle and other plunder.

He detailed eight men, including the wounded ones, to take the cattle, the poorest horses, and the prisoners, back to their home. There the children would be brought up as Chiricahuas, and in time, as usually happened, would become warriors and members of the tribe. The women would begin as slaves, but they would probably end by marrying Chiricahuas, and then they, too, joined the tribe.

Almost everyone took slaves in the Southwest in those days. There is some question about how this started. Very likely the early Spanish conquerors started it, as it was their practice to capture slaves whom they shipped down into Mexico to be sold.

In Cochise's time both the Mexicans and the Spanish-Americans who lived to the north, mercilessly took women and children as slaves from the Apaches. Some of the Pueblo Indians also owned Apache slaves.

The Apaches, in return, did the same thing to these enemies. Some of these captives, on both sides, were very unhappy; sometimes they were badly treated. The surprising thing is that many seem to have adjusted to their situation, and ended by joining the people who had been their deadly enemies. Indeed, Cochise's first wife was the daughter of a Mexican woman whom Mangas Coloradas had captured and married.

When the detachment had set off triumphantly to the north, the main body of warriors fed, watered, and rested their horses. They kept a sharp watch, ready to act if anyone should come towards San Felipe, but no one did. On the next day the war party set out for Ocotal.

CHAPTER VI

ONCE AGAIN COCHISE COUNTED on surprise, but this attack would be much more serious business. There was a strong garrison, and in addition, there were probably a hundred men living in the village, all of whom had arms and knew how to use them.

The garrison lived in a sort of fort, a building with thick, adobe walls built in a solid square around a court. The windows were narrow, half windows, half loopholes. The entrance had a heavy, double-door, which could not easily be broken down.

Ocotal was a fairly big village. There were always people moving about outside, rounding up horses, tending cattle, or hunting. Scouting it had to be done carefully. Cochise's scouts studied the place through one afternoon, watched it that night, and again through the morning.

They reported that during the day the cavalry's horses grazed in a meadow with a couple of men watching them. At night they were put in a corral outside the fort. There was a special bunch of eleven horses, very fine ones, that grazed separately in a place where the grass was green and plentiful. An old man, a civilian, watched over them. At night he drove them into the fort. Probably these horses belonged to the commander and some of the other high officers.

As an ordinary thing, the Apache chief would have planned a fast swoop. His warriors would have run off as many horses as possible, attacked a few outlying houses to get blankets, weapons, and gunpowder. They would have rounded up any cattle they encountered, and made off before a real fight could be organized. But this time, Cochise was bent on punishment. He wanted to give Mexico a lesson. He thought out a scheme.

The old man who had charge of the special horses seemed to know a great deal about the care of animals. The scouts noted that he was not alert, and that he was slow-moving. During part of the first afternoon they watched the old man go to sleep. He seemed to have no fear that the horses would leave their good grass to wander off into the barren desert.

On the next afternoon, when the old man woke from his nap, his horses were gone. He started up in great alarm. "Something must have frightened them," he muttered to himself. He picked up their tracks, and saw where they had gone into the desert to the west. They seemed to have traveled fairly steadily; certainly they were not in sight. The man did not go to get help, since he did not want the commander to know that he had neglected his duty.

The sun was setting and he was weary when he saw the horses again, huddled in a bend of some cliffs, where there was a small seep of water and some fair grass. He hurried to them, reproaching them in a low voice as he drew near. The horses knew him, and they were docile. He caught the leader and slipped a rope over his head, then he caught another horse, and on that one put the bridle he carried with him.

With the leader in hand, he did not need to worry about the other horses. They would always follow where the "top horse" went. They came along willingly, for the sun was down, and it was past time for them to enter the fort and receive their daily ration of corn.

The old man was puzzled about their behavior. It almost seemed as though someone, or something, had been holding the horses in that place, until he arrived. He had mostly been watching the horses' tracks, but he had also looked around for the tracks of humans, and he had seen none. It was dark before he reached the level, trampled ground near the fort. He did not see first one, then another dark shape separate itself from a bush, or rise from the ground, and melt in among the horses.

At the gate, the sentry growled at him for being late. It was past the hour when the main gate should be barred. The old man hurried in. The horses crowded together in the gateway, then moved in a bunch to the corner where they always received their grain and where hay was set out for them in a manger.

The sentry turned back to the gate. The old man went to get the corn. Though there were lights showing through doors and windows, much of the courtyard was dark. The troops were at their evening meal. The shadowy figures, five of them, slipped away from among the horses and hid in the haystack which stood back of the manger.

*   *   *

Again it was the first beginning of dawn. Again, small, harmless animals and birds gave their calls outside. Four of the five men stole away from the haystack. Two went to the gate, two to the door of the long room in which most of the troops slept. When they were in position, the fifth man struck a quick spark with flint and steel, and set fire to the haystack. At the same instant, the sentry at the door was pulled down.

The door was opened. Chiricahuas poured quietly into the fort. Another sentry, on the roof, gave the alarm of fire. Sleepy men began coming out of one door and another. Some carried their weapons, then seeing the fire, set them down here and there. Others came out unarmed.

The Chiricahuas were led by the men who had spent the night inside and who had

learned something of the layout. A file of warriors rushed for the racks where the guns stood lined up. Suddenly a soldier screamed, *"Apaches! Están los Apaches adentro!"* Then the fight began.

A good many of the soldiers got to their arms. The fighting was sharp. By no means all the Chiricahuas were free to attend to the troops. A group was assigned to get the fine horses out of the fort, another to run off the rest of the cavalry horses outside. Yet other groups swooped upon the houses and corrals of the civilians, for whatever plunder they could get.

Cochise intended to give Mexico a lesson, but he knew that he could not hope to wipe out the garrison. At a signal from him, the Chiricahuas broke off the fight in the fort. Within a few minutes, no Apaches remained in Ocotal. They assembled at a point he had chosen, where some men waited in reserve along with the novices. They brought with them their dead and wounded, and, again at Cochise's orders, a soldier prisoner.

They withdrew to a point about five miles from the village. There Cochise had the soldier brought to him. The man fully expected to be killed.

The chief addressed him through his interpreter. "Sixteen of your men came into my country, scalping women and little children. So we have come into your country to show you what we can do. Tell your chief to keep his men in Mexico, or we shall kill them all."

They removed all the soldier's clothing and turned him loose, deeply thankful to be alive. Then they headed towards home.

It had been a good raid. In addition to what they got at San Felipe, they had now taken more than a hundred horses, some mules, and fifty head of cattle. They had captured guns and ammunition and various other items of booty. They had killed at least twenty more soldiers.

The raid had not been without cost. Five warriors were dead. Cochise would have to call out five names before the tribe for the last time.

You had to expect to lose men when you went raiding, yet every loss disturbed Cochise. His nephew and one other had now served their fourth time as novices; they had become warriors. So five were lost and two were gained, and perhaps others would be lost before the three younger novices were ready for fighting.

Always he thought of the thousands and thousands of White-Eyes flooding the land and the fewness of the Chiricahuas. Not by means of numbers could he keep his people free in their own homeland. He put his trust in Yusn, the eternal. He called on Yusn in his heart for those other strengths that cannot be seen or counted.

CHAPTER VII

THE YEAR RAN OUT. IT WAS January, 1861, and Colonel Morrison still had taken no action to recover Miguel. John Ward was constantly after him, angry and insulting. Ward tried to raise a party of civilians to go after Cochise, but no one would join him. Finally, late in January, Colonel Morrison acted.

There had just arrived at Fort Buchanan a new officer, Second-Lieutenant George N. Bascom. Lieutenant Bascom was slight and blond. He wore a small, yellow mustache on his upper lip. He had a high opinion of himself. He had finished at West Point two years before, and had been on garrison duty at posts in the safe and peaceful East. He longed for service in the field; he wanted to earn promotion and fame.

This young officer pressed his colonel to give him the first active duty against the Indians that came along. Colonel Morrison was shortly able to oblige him.

Not long after Bascom had arrived at the fort, a detachment of cavalry returned there. It was commanded by Sergeant Reuben F. Bernard, a man who had already gained some fame as an Indian fighter.

Like many of those who fought Indians most successfully, the sergeant had taken the trouble to learn something about them. He understood them better and had more sympathy with them than most white men of those days. He was a big, solid man, deeply tanned by the western sun.

Colonel Morrison told Bascom about the kidnapping of little Miguel. "By now," he said, "the oxen the Indians took from Ward's ranch will have all been eaten. It's doubtful if the horses can be found."

But Morrison explained that the lieutenant was to do what he could to get the boy back.

He was to find out whether Cochise had made the raid, and if so, try to negotiate with him. The colonel made it clear that the Chiricahuas were supposed not to be on the warpath, and he described the nature of Ward's evidence. Bascom would have fifty-four soldiers and an interpreter, and Ward would go with him.

The expedition set out on the 29th of January, reaching the Overland Mail Station at Apache Pass on February 3rd. Along the way, Bascom had plenty of time to plan. He was one of those officers who felt it part of his duty to keep his men in their places.

Bernard was an enlisted man, not an officer, so the lieutenant did not talk with him except when necessary. Thus he missed a chance to learn a little something about Indians, and especially about Apaches, other than the wild tales he had heard in the East. He talked more with Ward. Probably Ward filled him full of all the worst stories about Cochise. Ward certainly convinced the greenhorn lieutenant that the Chiricahuas had stolen Miguel.

In Bascom's opinion all Indians were liars, thieves, cowards, and murderers. He did not quite hold that they should all be wiped out. But he was convinced that the only argument that they could understand was force, and if necessary, brutality. He was sure that it was simply silly to think that any Apache chief would keep the peace, no matter what promises he had made.

Colonel Morrison had told him to negotiate with Cochise. He did not like that word, "negotiate." It meant to come to some kind of agreement by persuasion. He did not see how anyone could persuade savages and he considered that compromising with them was unworthy of an officer and a gentleman. He was not exactly sure what he was going to do, but he hoped for a chance to teach Cochise a lesson he wouldn't forget.

The day was warm and sunny. What wind there was blew from the south. There was snow on the tops of the mountains, but in Apache Pass it was like spring. The detachment rode along easily. Sergeant Bernard, from old experience, had his scouts out and kept a sharp watch himself. He took it for granted that the Apaches were watching them, which did not occur to the lieutenant.

They rode up to the Station in the middle of the afternoon. Several of the Apaches' dome-shaped huts stood about six hundred yards from the Station. The Chiricahuas who supplied wood and hay lived in these.

Bascom eyed the Indians curiously. They were the first he had seen, and it surprised him to find savages living as neighbors to white men, with no troops to control them. Had the lieutenant not already made up his mind, he would have seen how everything pointed to peace with the Chiricahuas. Near the huts, children were playing.

There were only three men at the Station: Culver, who was in charge, Walsh, the hostler, and Wallace, a stage driver. These men were neither pleased nor displeased to see soldiers arriving; they simply were surprised. It had been a long time since any troops had passed that way.

"We're just passing through," Bascom told the three men, after he had arranged for the horses to be watered. "I wanted to rest the horses, so I'll camp over there in the valley." He pointed to a small depression east of the Station. Then he said casually to Culver, "Since I'm going to stop here for a while, I'd like to see this Cochise I've heard so much about. I think it would be interesting to talk with him. Do you think he's likely to turn up?"

Culver knew very well that the Apaches would have been watching the troop, and Cochise would have heard by now that they were camping here. He would certainly be curious, and he would be likely to come to the Station.

"Likely he'll be around a little later," Culver answered.

"Tell Cochise I'd like to meet him, if you see him," Bascom said with a show of casualness. "Tell him I'm putting a white flag in front of my tent."

"All right," Culver agreed. "If the chief comes, I'll tell him."

The soldiers mounted and rode off to a good camping site, about a quarter of a mile beyond the Station. Bascom had a white flag put up. The story he told Culver shows that he had already made his plans, and they were not the plans of a frank and honest man.

The three civilians talked the matter over. They were rather puzzled. It was reasonable enough that soldiers should be moving towards the Río Grande where, between Mangas Coloradas' Apaches and their allies, there was plenty of fighting to be done. The early camp could also be understood, allowing

for the slow way soldiers travel. The lieutenant had probably been told that it was a
good distance further on before water could
be found.

What was odd was this business about
wanting to talk to Cochise! What business
could a tenderfoot second-lieutenant have with
the chief of the Chiricahuas? If you wanted
to do anything with Cochise you'd send the
highest ranking officer from the fort. Culver
and his companions concluded that the lieutenant had merely spoken out of curiosity.
Maybe Cochise would visit him. If so, the
lieutenant ought to feel honored.

Bascom meanwhile instructed some of his
men to surround his tent, if and when Cochise
should visit him. He ordered them to see
to it that the Apache did not get away unless
he, Bascom, gave permission. Apparently he
told Sergeant Bernard nothing about this
scheme.

On the following morning Cochise came to
the Station, to find out what soldiers were
doing in the Pass. He brought with him his
second wife and their son, still a small boy.
He also brought Thin Man, his brother and
counsellor, Mesquite, and another, slightly
older nephew.

Since the day was even milder than the day before, the men wore only their breechclouts and moccasins. The Apache breechclout was a long, wide piece of material pulled through a belt. The ends hung down in front and behind as far as the wearer's knees or further. The party carried no weapons, except that Cochise wore a knife. He was not carrying this as a weapon, but almost as part of his clothing. It was fastened to his belt in front, and hidden by the fold of his breechclout.

Cochise asked about the soldiers. Wallace, who spoke fair Apache, said that they were on their way to the Río Grande and would probably break camp soon. He passed on Bascom's message, including the remark about the white flag.

Cochise was always suspicious of white men he did not know. At once he wondered if anything lay behind this invitation. Could it be a trap? He talked it over with his brother.

"The new chief of the White-Eyes who has taken Steen's place has sent this sub-chief to see you," Thin Man suggested, "to renew the promise of friendship and peace." Cochise had been hoping for some such development. He was pleased.

The Chiricahuas walked over to the camp. Cochise saw the white flag, set up as Wallace had told him. Then he was sure that all was well. He led his party confidently past the soldiers, directly to the tent, where Bascom and Ward awaited him. The Indians filed in and arranged themselves on the ground in silence. They waited as usual for a time before anything could be said.

Bascom waited, too. He was arranging his thoughts, planning his words, thinking ahead. Also, he was studying the chief just as the chief was studying him.

They made a strange impression on each other. Cochise saw an officer who, it seemed to him, was not yet a man. He studied Bascom's face, red with sunburn after his days in the saddle. He saw the little, blond mustache which failed to give maturity to his mouth. It did not please Cochise that a child like this should be sent to speak with him.

Bascom could hardly believe that the man before him was the famous chief. The soldier was too young, and too prejudiced against Indians, to see Cochise's dignity or his expression of strength and thoughtfulness. All he saw was a half-naked savage with none of the trappings he had expected.

The woman with Cochise was rather good-looking but the way her hair hung loose all over her shoulders, he thought, showed that the women were just as savage as the men. Not a one of the party wore even a single feather. He was disappointed.

Outside the tent, he knew, his men had moved silently into position. He felt his heart beat a little faster. He was going to get back Ward's boy; he was going to succeed. Now he must be careful. He cleared his throat and began speaking in a pompous voice, pausing now and again while the interpreter translated.

He described the raid on Ward's ranch and stated that he knew the Chiricahuas had made it. The young white chief told about the boy. Then he said that he wanted the boy and the stolen horses returned immediately.

To Cochise, Bascom sounded as if he were giving orders, although the interpreter softened the pompous tone and the words. Cochise felt himself getting angry, but he held himself back. When Bascom finished, there was a long silence.

Cochise was thinking hard. He had been doubly insulted, by being accused of breaking his word, and by being spoken to in such a manner by this immature child. Still, he could not allow himself to be angry. Great trouble could be made by fools like this. It was necessary to explain to the soldier, to straighten him out. As chief of the Chiricahuas, he must see to it that nothing threatened their peace with the White-Eyes.

Carefully and patiently he explained that ever since he and the chief they called Steen had become friends, there had been friendship between the Chiricahuas and the White-Eyes. He had pledged his word, and everyone knew that he never broke a pledge.

For five years, relations had been peaceful; his people had made no raids in the White-Eyes' country; they had stolen no horses. On the contrary, they had protected the mail coaches and worked for the Station.

As for this kidnapped boy, he had never heard of him. He knew nothing about him or the horses. He would, however, be glad to help find him. He could ask among the other Apache tribes, and if he learned where the boy was, he would do what he could to get the child back.

It was plain that Bascom did not believe Cochise. He kept on asking the Indians to produce the boy. Cochise, his brother, and his older nephew controlled their tempers. They went over the same ground again and again.

One cannot help but wonder just what was going on in Bascom's prejudiced mind. He knew that there was some doubt whether the Chiricahuas had stolen Miguel. He knew that Cochise had, at least, seemed to keep the peace for five years.

Certainly, the Overland Mail Station had been peacefully maintained in Apache Pass, in the heart of the Chiricahua country. In all that time no troops had been needed to defend it. It ought to have been clear that Cochise wanted to continue at peace.

A man who knew something about Indians would have been inclined to accept Cochise's offer to try to find the boy, even if he still believed that the Chiricahuas had stolen the child. Such a man would have figured that the chief would not want to admit that his people had made that raid. The offer accepted, Cochise would say after a short time that he had found the boy among some other group.

A man who had experience with the Apaches would have known that Cochise spoke nothing but the truth and would have believed him. In either case, he would have been content at least for the moment with what Cochise said.

In addition, anyone familiar with the situation would have wanted to avoid doing anything that might put the Chiricahuas on the warpath. There was trouble enough in the Southwest without stirring them up.

Talk that has to be interpreted is always slow. This talk had gone on for a long time. The Indians were getting more and more disturbed and angry, but, following Cochise's lead, they kept an appearance of calmness.

Finally, Bascom decided to bring the debate to an end. He said to the interpreter, "Tell Cochise that I know very well he is lying. I hold all these people hostages, and I shall hold them until they bring back Ward's son."

The interpreter hesitated before he translated this. He knew there was going to be trouble of some kind. Finally, he put the words into Apache.

There was a moment of stillness. Then Cochise leaped to his feet, whipping out his knife. His eyes blazed, his face was full of fury. He gave a wild cry, then called to his

people, "Follow me!" He leaped across the tent, slit the canvas wall open and jumped out.

His brother and the older nephew jumped after him. Cochise had taken the guards by complete surprise; if there was to be a break, they expected it to be through the door. He got past them. Some of them fired at him. He ran twisting and turning from side to side. A bullet grazed his leg, but he got away.

Thin Man and the nephew were not so lucky. A soldier knocked Thin Man down with the butt of his rifle; Cochise's nephew was bayoneted in the stomach. Mesquite never got beyond the wall of the tent. He saw it was useless, and he ran back.

The white flag had been violated, the peace had been broken.

CHAPTER VIII

COCHISE PAID NO ATTENTION at all to his wound. He ran to the little settlement of Apaches near the Station, warned them of trouble, and sent the few men there to get more. He moved to a hiding place for the moment, lest the Americans should come after him while he was alone and unarmed. There he thought over the situation.

This young soldier chief with the little mustache could not be an important one. He was plainly stupid and ignorant. Probably the principal chief, at the fort, had no idea what the young one was doing. There was hope that this would not be a cause for war. The thing to do was to get his relatives back, and then try to see the high chief, or send him a message.

The best way, Cochise decided, to make the soldiers release their prisoners would be to capture some hostages for himself. He waited until about twenty of his warriors, all armed, had gathered, which they did in a few minutes. Then he took them to a place within calling distance of the Mail Station. He thought, rightly, that the people there would not yet know what had happened. Standing on a slight rise of ground, Cochise called "Culver!" He called several times.

Culver came out, and Walsh appeared in the doorway. Cochise motioned Culver to him. Out of curiosity, Walsh came along, too. When the two men reached the group of Indians, the warriors jumped to seize them. The white men grappled. They were strong. They broke free and ran for the Station.

The Indians were excited and angry; they were more than ready for a fight. As the white men ran, they opened fire, and Culver was shot down.

*   *   *

After Cochise got away, Sergeant Bernard
managed to persuade the lieutenant to order
his troops to the Station, which could be
defended, and to put the hostages there under
guard.   The troops came at double quick
time from one side, as Culver and Walsh were

racing towards the Station from the other. The soldiers saw the Apache warriors on the high ground, and they heard the shots. They did not see Walsh running toward safety.

Walsh got to the wall of the corral and started to scramble over it. Excited soldiers had run into the corral, ready for an attack. When they saw someone coming over the top, they shot before they could see that the man was not an Indian. Walsh fell back, on the outside of the wall.

When Cochise saw that the Station was garrisoned, he moved his men back out of gun range. He ordered them to watch the place. He would go to the East Stronghold, to think out the problems alone. As he rode along, he met two groups of his fighting men coming up. The leader of one, a fierce warrior ever hungry for fighting, told him that a wagon train was camped in the Pass.

Cochise said, "Good. Take it, and bring me back any White-Eyes in the wagon train. Bring them alive and uninjured."

His lieutenant did not like the last part of the order, but the rest pleased him greatly.

Cochise sent another party to attack the stagecoach, which was due shortly. He gave its leader instructions to break down the bridge the coach would have to cross and to bring in as many live White-Eyes as possible.

Then the chief went on alone to the East Stronghold, to sit meditating through the night. It was not easy for Cochise to think clearly and calmly at that point, however he might try to send his thoughts towards Yusn, the Life-Giver.

The situation of his wife, his child, his brother, his nephews, filled him with anger and fear. As every Apache knows, anger and fear are two of the emotions that do most to cloud the mind and weaken the spirit.

The memory of Bascom filled him with anger, anger for the insults he had had to swallow, for the stupidity, the childishness of the man. It was all so foolish, so unnecessary. He knew nothing of this kidnapped boy, nothing of the raid on Ward's ranch.

Then from the soldier's stupidity, had sprung the threat of war, much greater now that two White-Eyes were dead. He had not wanted to hurt them, only to use them to trade for his own people. He hoped still to quiet this matter, but he did not know if he could do it.

While the chief meditated, the two war

parties went about their business. The group to attack the stagecoach took positions by a small bridge. Cochise had told them to destroy part of the bridge, so that the coach could not pass, but they seem not to have understood, or else they simply did not understand about bridges. They took out a plank, but left the bridge still usable. Then they hid themselves to right and left of the road.

The coach, pulled by six mules, came along from Tucson at a trot. When it had almost reached the bridge, the Apaches opened fire, killing one lead mule and wounding the driver. It happened that William Buckley, the superintendent of the mail service, was on the coach. He quickly took the driver's place. While he and some of the passengers opened fire, two others leaped out, cut the dead mule free, and raced back into the coach.

The superintendent lashed the mules into a wild run. The coach crossed the bridge. The mules jumped the broken part, and were going so fast that they jerked the coach over safely. The Apaches followed the coach to the Station, exchanging shots with the passengers. No shots hit their mark and when the Indians came within range of the soldiers, they fell back.

As Buckley drew rein beside the Station, the terrified passengers ran inside.

The people with the wagon train had no such luck. The war party sent after them waited until they were peacefully asleep, then fell upon them. There was no chance for a fight.

The Chiricahuas found two Americans, whom they took prisoner as Cochise had ordered. They also found some Mexicans, and these they killed. They plundered and burned the wagons and drove off the stock.

William Buckley was an experienced frontiersman. He hated Indians, but he did not underrate them. It was clear to him that serious trouble had started.

He thought that the force at the Mail Station might well find itself attacked by the full strength of the Chiricahuas. He also decided that Bascom was something of a fool. He persuaded the lieutenant to let him send out a courier to the stage line's agent in Tuscon. In a letter to the agent he described the situation, and ordered him to get help to the Station as soon as possible.

Bascom was not concerned; he rather liked the thought of a fight. After all, he had never seen combat. He did see that the fight might be a hard one, and it occurred to him that he could use a surgeon. So he sent another courier to Colonel Morrison, asking that one be provided for him. Both messengers got through.

In the morning Cochise came again to the rise of ground, accompanied by the captured white men from the wagon train and by a number of his men. One of the warriors carried a white flag. Apparently the chief had not yet given up his faith in the white man's respect for a flag of truce.

Cochise called for Wallace, the third man who lived at the Station. Wallace spoke Apache; his relations with Cochise had been friendly. The chief had some faith in him.

Several people pleaded with Wallace not to answer, but Wallace insisted on going out into the corral where he was within easy speaking range.

Cochise said, "I have two Americans here. Tell that soldier that I will give them to him if he will give me back my people."

Wallace gave the message to Bascom. The lieutenant got angry. He said that he would hang all the Indians if Cochise did not release the men immediately. Wallace, Sergeant Bernard, and some of the civilians from the coach argued with him. Finally the lieutenant said that he would release the hostages if the two American men and Ward's boy were returned. Wallace thought it useless to deliver any such message. He determined to go out and talk to Cochise himself.

Cochise was waiting anxiously for an answer. If the exchange could be made, then there was still hope that the other difficulties could be talked out. He was deeply concerned about his relatives, his wife, his child. He saw their faces in memory, remembered Thin Man's wise counsels, young Mesquite just become a man. His heart was in a turmoil. He was feeling violent emotions that he could not entirely master.

He watched Wallace come out of the door and walk toward him. He had thought of Wallace as a friend, but he realized suddenly that it was Wallace who had first lied to him about where the troops were going and what they wanted. All White-Eyes were alike! They were all liars; none of them could be trusted.

Wallace stood before him. "I tell you plainly, I cannot get the young soldier chief to give up the hostages. He still believes that the Chiricahuas kidnapped

Ward's boy. The soldier will not turn his captives loose until the boy has been returned."

Wallace planned to say much more. He was hoping to talk Cochise into waiting. He hoped somehow to stave off violent action on either side, and bring about an understanding. Especially, he hoped to bring into the affair, men of more rank and wisdom than Bascom. The white man and Cochise, then, were thinking alike, but they never found it out.

When Cochise heard the first part of what Wallace had to say, anger overcame him. This unknown boy again! This impossible demand which he was helpless to satisfy! Why should he allow himself to be insulted? Why should his wife and child and the others be held prisoners?

"Then I take you, too," he growled. As he spoke, one of his men lassoed Wallace and they dragged him off.

Thereafter Cochise would have no speech with this captive, being convinced that he was a traitor. Anger piled on anger, event upon event, until hatred had overthrown reason and there was no room for anything but war.

CHAPTER IX

THE CHIRICAHUAS DID NOT FEEL strong enough to attack the Station directly. It was too well-suited for defense and too well-manned with men whose ability to fight they respected as they did not that of the Mexicans. Cochise, also, still wanted to avoid a battle. His plan was to hold the place under quiet siege. He thought that he could show the child chief, as he called him, that he had made a mistake.

Then, perhaps, the White-Eyes would become reasonable and release the captives.

After that, the siege could be lifted and they could negotiate.

Between the troops and the Overland Mail, a large number of horses and mules were being held in the corral. Cochise saw that the water supply was bound to run out, and the animals would have to be taken to the springs for water. He prepared for that. On the fourth day after his escape from the tent, a party of soldiers and civilians escorted the horses and mules to the springs.

A detachment of Chiricahuas attacked. They killed one American, wounded two others, and ran off a considerable part of the stock. Only a small number of the Indians was engaged in this fight. Cochise could easily have sent fifty or a hundred men, some to engage the garrison with a holding attack, the rest to wipe out the party and take all the stock.

Cochise was a skillful strategist; he could have handled such a situation neatly. But he was trying to give warning and teach the Americans a lesson rather than start a full-scale war. Also, his warriors were hampered in the fighting by further instructions to take prisoners, which they failed to do.

Cochise was torn, divided in mind and heart. He was thoroughly angry. When he thought of the captives his heart sickened. Still he clung to the hope of avoiding war.

Yet that hope was getting slim; perhaps war was already here. If so, as a good general he knew that he should strike first, with all his power. Further, all his people, all his counsellors, clamored for war. It was extraordinary that he held them back as long as he did.

The day after the raid on the horses, Cochise appeared again on the rise of ground. Again he used a white flag, and was accompanied only by a relatively small number of warriors. They brought Wallace with them. Wallace was cold and hungry; his face was drawn. The Chiricahuas had not mistreated him, but they had wasted no kindness on him.

Wallace called out to Bascom, begging him to exchange the Indian hostages for the Americans held by Cochise. Wallace urged as hard as he knew how, but Bascom refused to budge. He would not release his hostages until Cochise produced Ward's adopted boy.

Wallace tried to argue with him, but the officer simply cut off the talk, and walked back into the Station. He acted as though he was proud of showing firmness. Probably he thought that he was being clever in not letting the Apache chief deceive him. He certainly did not see that if Cochise did not produce one small boy, it must be because Cochise did not have him!

Two days later, Cochise tried again. This time he presented himself differently. It was time, he decided, to make it perfectly clear to the child chief that the full power of the Chiricahuas was assembled and ready to move.

He gathered his warriors, and arrayed himself in his finest war gear. He painted his face in several colors, put on a buckskin shirt decorated with shells and charms, wrapped a fine blanket around his waist. He attached eagle plumes to the side of his headband. He mounted his best horse. Then, with Wallace tied to a rope and led by one of his warriors, he brought a large part of his whole force to confront the men in the Station.

It was a sight to make any sensible, practical man think twice. The armed, mounted, war-painted warriors appeared suddenly all along the ridge. The line reached to the left and right until trees hid its flanks. An observer could not tell just how long it was. The men

were well-armed. Most carried bows and
lances, but a great many had guns.

Bascom, looking through his field glasses,
could see that some of these guns were old
muskets, but that some were rifles of recent
make. In the center, Cochise sat his horse,
a splendid, and at the same time a truly

savage figure.   A slight distance ahead of him was Wallace, on a lead-rope.

This time Wallace pleaded desperately with Bascom to exchange hostages.   He said that he had not eaten in several days.   He and the other captives said that they could not hold out much longer.   Bascom, unmoved, stubbornly gave the same old answer.   Some of the civilians about him murmured, but that only made the young West-Pointer the more stubborn.

Cochise watched and listened intently.   He knew only a few words of English, but he was beginning to recognize the words "boy" or "Ward's boy."   Understanding words or not, he could read faces and recognize tones.   All he had to do was to listen to Wallace's pleading.

It was clear that the child chief had not changed his mind.   Cochise tried to throw his thought into the heart of that little man down there, to understand him, but he could not. Everything he did was unreasonable; he was the kind of man one could not understand.

"Somehow," the Indian chief said to himself, "I must try to bring this talking to a point.   I cannot go on like this forever.   I cannot stand it, and my fighting men will not hold back forever."

In a low voice he said to a sub-chief who sat his horse on his right, "Tell the White-Eyes that this is the last time I will come here to talk. I have offered to trade these men for my people; I shall not make the offer again."

The sub-chief, speaking in a louder voice, passed the message to Wallace.

Wallace translated Cochise's words. Then he said, "In the name of God, Mr. Bascom, exchange us! Don't you see, if you don't, this is the end of us?"

Bascom said, angrily, "I have told you, I'll exchange when he brings the Ward boy. That's flat. Tell him."

"I can't tell him that, lieutenant. It wouldn't do no good. He ain't got no boy, don't you understand? He don't know nothin' about him. In the name of God, lieutenant!"

Several of the civilians interfered, urging Bascom to make the exchange. Sergeant Bernard joined in, putting his arguments forcefully. That an enlisted man should interfere with an officer made Bascom angry. After a few words he placed the sergeant under arrest, to be tried for insubordination.

The people around him made it clear that Bascom was sending Wallace and the two unknown men from the wagon train to their deaths. Worse, they were abandoning them to the cruel modes of death one might expect at the hands of profoundly angry Apaches.

None of this moved the officer. He saw himself in a heroic role. He must prove that he, Second Lieutenant George N. Bascom, U. S. A., was stronger than that savage chief up there.

He felt that if he gave in, he would be showing weakness to the Indians. He could see well enough that Cochise badly wanted to get his relatives back. It did not occur to him that if a stray six-year-old boy was all that was needed to free the hostages, Cochise would gladly produce him if he could.

Bascom threw back his shoulders and struck a military position. He called out in a firm voice, "I stand on what I said. I'll make the exchange when he produces the Ward boy."

Cochise had continued watching, listening. He watched the debate down there in the corral, heard the voices faintly. It amazed him that this youth, this mustached child, did not have to listen to the older, more experienced men who argued with him. No Apache chief would go so against his older counsellors—but then, no one like that could ever have become an Apache chief. No one would follow him.

He saw that the child chief had ended the argument, breaking it off. He heard him call to Wallace. All he needed to do was watch Wallace's face, whether or not he caught the words, "Ward boy," again. He heard Wallace begin to plead once more. His keen eyes read the set, stubborn, not-listening expression of the child chief.

Clearly, further talk could gain nothing. Cochise gave an order, and as he did so, wheeled his horse. All the Indians turned away. They rode off, dragging their captive after them.

When they reached a stopping place, the warriors took it for granted that the time had come to abandon this odd custom of keeping grown, male captives alive. Cochise did not care. He let them do as they pleased. The three men were killed with brutality. Then their bodies were left to the buzzards.

Cochise detailed men to keep watch on the Mail Station and make it dangerous for anyone to leave it, others to watch the Pass and close it to traffic. He wanted time to consult with the old men, with the medicine men, and with the leaders under him. He still wanted time to think. If this was to be war, it would be a big, serious, deadly war; it would need planning.

The Chiricahuas had treated their hostages barbarously. The white men were not doing much better. They had a woman and a child, one healthy young warrior, a warrior who had been seriously wounded in the stomach, and a middle-aged sick man who had been smashed in the chest by a gun butt. They simply threw these people into a dark room and locked them in. From time to time they pushed in some food and water, that was all.

The wounded man was in bad shape, probably slowly dying, and Thin Man spat blood from time to time. The mother comforted her child; the little boy did his best to behave as a man and a Chiricahua.

It almost seems as if the two sides were competing to see who could do the worst. White men at the time justified their acts by pointing to the deeds of their enemies. This was not a very good argument for people who proudly stated that they were civilized and Christian, and that the Apaches were ignorant savages. It is not by his enemies but by himself and his own standards that a man of honor judges his acts.

*   *   *

Three days later Cochise's scouts advised him that strong reinforcements were coming to the Station. They were already in Chiricahua country and would probably reach the Station next day. These consisted, as a matter of fact, of two troops of cavalry, a large body of civilians led by the Mail Line Agent from Tucson, and a small detachment of infantry accompanying a military surgeon from Fort Buchanan.

The scouts, watching the three groups, reported that the foot soldiers had run across a small party of Coyotero Apaches returning from a raid, and had captured three of them. This news interested the Chiricahuas only slightly, except that it showed that the man in command of that party was a clever fighter.

The Coyoteros lived far to the north, farther than the Pinaleños. Many of their ways were different from the Chiricahuas', and in the past the two tribes had had a number of fights. Cochise had no time to worry about them.

If he were sure that war had started, he could attack these groups, one by one, before they assembled. There would be hard fighting, but they could probably be driven back. Many of his counsellors wanted to do just that, especially the younger leaders.

Finally, they accepted Cochise's counsel, which was to wait. With all these white men Cochise hoped there might well be a wiser, older chief, someone really responsible, with whom he could talk. The young men grumbled; they clamored for combat. For a while yet, they were willing to obey.

Cochise realized that when all these reinforcements were together with the men at the Station, there would be a powerful force. To play safe, he sent word for the women and children to abandon their settlement of well-built houses and move into camp. He took the main body of his own force to a position a little further away from the Station, where, if need be, he could most easily cover the women's retreat to the East Stronghold.

He would not himself, at this point, go seeking speech with the White-Eyes. He would stay here, keep his scouts out, and wait. He would not come pleading to the soldiers at the Station, not even for those he loved.

Once again, what Cochise wanted almost happened. On the next day, the fifteenth of February, all the troops and the civilians were assembled at the Station. First Lieutenant Moore of the cavalry took command.

He was older than Bascom and much more experienced. His first move was to try to negotiate with Cochise. To this end, he rode with a strong party to the thatched homes of the Chiricahua ranchería, not knowing it was abandoned. On his way, he happened to pass by where the bodies of Wallace and the other two men lay.

The buzzards had been at them for some time. Moore and his men could plainly see how barbarously these three had been killed. The officer was deeply shocked and filled with anger. He abandoned the thought of negotiating. It seemed to him that Cochise must be fully on the warpath.

There would be no use in talking with him, little or no hope that a talk could be arranged. Instead of trying to arrange a meeting, the soldier found and burned the empty huts.

No one needed to tell Cochise that the ranchería had been set on fire; he could see the smoke. It did not surprise him, but it ended his last hope of peace. He assembled his leaders to start planning at once not only for defense, but for attack. Scouts brought him news that all the troops were leaving the Station, moving west. Then scouts brought him other, more poignant news.

When he heard the words of his scouts, Cochise mounted immediately, followed by most of his leaders and fighting men. He rode, not in the direction of the withdrawing White-Eyes, but towards the burned ranchería until he reached the place where Lieutenant Moore had found the three bodies.

The bodies of the White-Eyes had been buried, but to replace them, six other bodies swung, hanged from the limbs of an oak tree. They were his brother, his two nephews, and the three unknown Coyoteros.

Cochise made himself gaze upon the six until his mind encompassed the meaning of his loss. The hanging, along with the Chiricahuas, of these others from an alien tribe, helped to build his hate. The presence of those Coyoteros showed how aimlessly the White-Eyes killed. There was no more doubting; everything was clear. His heart steadied. He gave orders for the tribe to gather in the Stronghold, to hold the rituals for the beginning of full-scale, formal, deadly war.

CHAPTER X

LIEUTENANT MOORE WITH-
drew from Apache Pass for several good
reasons. He did not have enough strength
to undertake to pursue and attack the cursed
Chiricahuas in their own country. The
Station could not be held for long unless the
Pass could be opened again, so that supplies
could come through. To do that would take
a campaign by a large force. In fact, it would
almost require winning the war.

The civilians would not remain indefinitely.
And his own orders were only to relieve
Lieutenant Bascom, to see if he could settle the

difficulty, and return. It was clear that he could not settle it; now he was due to return.

The Americans got out of the Chiricahua country without seeing a single Apache—which did not necessarily mean there were none around. The cavalry under Moore returned to Fort Breckenridge, where they were stationed. Bascom took his men and those who had come with the surgeon, along with the two remaining captives, to Fort Buchanan.

At the fort, Colonel Morrison ordered Cochise's wife and child released. The Mexicans and Indians might go in for taking slaves, but he did not believe in making war on women and children. The two set out on foot to Chiricahua country.

Lieutenant Bascom had unleashed war with a determined and skillful enemy upon a country that already had all it could handle. His line of action had already cost the lives of six Americans—Culver, Walsh, and Wallace, the two men from the wagon train, and the man killed at the spring when they went to water the horses.

It had also cost the lives of the Mexicans who had been with the wagon train, and of the six Apaches, about whom nobody cared.

Further, he had not accomplished his mission. Yet, instead of being reprimanded, he was praised. The hanging of the six Apache prisoners met with official approval.

That approval gives evidence of the official attitude towards Apaches at that time. It was not much different from Bascom's own. The lives of Indians were considered to be of no value. It was believed that the only thing they understood was brutal force, and it was all right to lie to them or to violate a flag of truce.

Colonel Morrison did not seem upset over the trouble Bascom had started. He probably did not realize just how serious it was. The Americans had withdrawn from the Pass without any trouble at all. No attack had been made on their camps; not even a rifle shot or an arrow had come out of the darkness. No attempt was made to harass the troops as they marched.

Only a man who knew a great deal about the Chiricahuas would have guessed what this meant. Only such a man would have known that all but the fewest possible scouts were taking part in a great war ceremony. There may not have been any white man at that time who knew anything about such a ritual. Most likely no one knew that the ceremony encompassed a plan for the most deadly and constant war.

Colonel Morrison, then, concluded that the hanging of the six Apaches had had an excellent effect. Ward's boy had not been recovered, but it looked as if, all in all, between Bascom and Moore, Cochise had been given a fine lesson. Apparently the policy of firmness had paid, and the Apaches were cowed by it. Hence the hangings were approved and Bascom was not reprimanded.

But a month later, when Sergeant Bernard was tried on Bascom's charge of insubordination, things had changed. The sergeant was set free and sent back to his regiment. Good fighters were needed in the regiment. The American troops were up to their necks in trouble.

Far away in the East, the threat of war between the North and the South was looming. What Lieutenant Bascom had done did not look so clever, and the sergeant was too valuable a man to have penned up in a military prison.

*   *   *

While the troops withdrew, the Chiricahuas prepared their spirits for war. They did not dance violently, jump up and down, or yell. There was dancing, but it was solemn. There were many chanted prayers.

The warriors sought for omens. Knowing that they must maintain war against many times their numbers, they prayed for strength. They sought for the qualities within themselves that make one man equal to many, the qualities that come from Yusn.

Cochise sent messengers to Mangas Coloradas to say that at last he was ready to join his old friend and teacher. He would ally himself with Mangas' Red Paint People, commonly called the Mimbreños. He would even be an ally to the Mescaleros, the Pinaleños, and the Arivaipas, on whom the Chiricahuas had so often looked as enemies.

He would go so far as to be friendly with the Navajos, if that great tribe would join in the fight. He would fight side by side with friends and enemies among the Apaches to free all Apachería of White-Eyes, as long ago they had freed it of Mexicans.

The raids had hardly begun when scouts went to answer a smoke signal and found Cochise's wife and son. They brought them to the chief. His poignant joy at seeing them again, safe and whole, even though they were

hungry and very tired, was great. But he did not relax his determination to drive the White-Eyes out of the country.

This act of mercy on the part of Colonel Morrison, however, did have a profound effect upon Cochise, although it was years before that effect produced any result. The strange, unreasonable, withering experiences just past had closed his mind and heart completely against all White-Eyes.

Now his mind was opened a tiny crack. He had to entertain the thought that among them there was some decency. He had to admit to himself that there was some point at which they drew the line. Since war was declared, he would have thought it natural enough for his enemies to have kept his wife and child as slaves. Yet they had been set free to return home.

The war parties went out. They raided into the southeastern part of Arizona and the southwestern part of New Mexico. Their raids reached further and further. They harassed the troops, and when the soldiers came after them, set traps and ambushed them. Soon, the whole Southwest, and then the whole nation knew that the Chiricahuas were at war.

CHAPTER XI

THE AMERICANS IN THE EAST could read in the papers about Cochise and the Chiricahuas. Cochise had no way of knowing what happened in that far land. Neither he nor Mangas Coloradas knew that on the Atlantic coast the Southerners had captured Fort Sumter, and that a great war had started.

What the scouts reported about Apachería and the surrounding country was that, little by little, the soldiers were abandoning their posts. The garrisons had become few and far between.

The Indian chiefs thought that this was the result of their campaigns. They had raided the posts, cut off supply trains, killed many couriers, run off horses, captured arms. They had fought engagements with the troops, picking favorable chances, and had won many of them.

Their mode of warfare was generally hit-and-run. The Apaches traveled faster than even the best of the blue-coated cavalry, and could keep going much longer. They knew all the byways and side trails, and how to get through where there were no trails. They raided and ran, doing all the harm they could. They did not let themselves get caught in a regular battle except when they themselves arranged it.

Unlike many Indians, the Apaches looked upon warfare as a strictly practical matter; they had the same attitude as professional soldiers. Their aim was to defeat the enemy at the least cost to themselves, although when their time came, they were not afraid to die.

They wiped out ranches, they forced mines to close down. Mangas Coloradas was particularly determined to end all mining. "Where there is a mine," he explained to the younger chief, "a town is likely to grow up.

A mine brings a settlement of many White-Eyes, stronger, much harder to wipe out, than a ranch."

But there were other reasons for Mangas' hatred of mines, as Cochise well knew. When the old man spoke of these, his eyes burned. He was not a handsome man; his nose was too big, his face too broad. He was as tall as Cochise, and heavier, older, a powerful man in his sixties. When he thought of those other reasons, his eyes burned, his face darkened; he seemed like a thundercloud full of lightning inside.

When he was younger, before the White-Eyes had their war with the Mexicans, a group of the strangers had prepared a feast. They had joined with the people of a village called Santa Rita in inviting the chief of the Red Paint People. They had invited the chief and all of those Indians who wished to come, to attend.

They had spread out food and gifts for the Apaches. Then, when they were busy eating, they had opened fire upon them. They had killed more than two hundred men, women, and children, including the chief.

It was then that Mangas had become chief of the Mimbreños. The Americans had left

Santa Rita and got clean away, but Mangas made it his first business to wipe out the place. In a few months he had succeeded in his mission and Santa Rita became only a memory. That was the beginning of Mangas' long career of wars.

Then had come the white men's war with Mexico and after that, chiefs of the White-Eyes had sought him out and made peace with him. They spoke well to him and gave him gifts. He, like Cochise, had thought that some of them might be good, and that one could live quietly as their neighbors.

Then a party of five prospectors had come into the Mimbres country, the territory of the Red Paint People. As usual, they were looking for the yellow metal, the mere thought of which seemed to drive white men crazy. Mangas had not wanted them in his territory, but he had not wanted to make trouble, so he had visited their camp. He told them about a place, outside the Mimbres borders, where he himself had seen the yellow metal.

The Americans had been drinking. They did not believe him. They decided to have some fun. They seized Mangas Coloradas, tied him to a tree, and beat him until he knew nothing that was going on. He, as a good Apache, had made no sound while they were beating him.

When he came to, the White-Eyes had gone. He had worked free of the ropes and gone to get his warriors. Four of these five prospectors they had killed; the fifth had escaped, and made his way north, to Santa Fe, where he had told the story. It was a story that Mangas also told on occasion.

Talking with Cochise, he said that he was happy that now his younger brother, too, had learned that the White-Eyes were altogether bad. The only thing to do was to let none of them remain within Apachería. Together they would drive the last of their enemies out of the land, and their country would be free once more.

Cochise listened quietly. He had no love for the White-Eyes, but he had known one or two who had been good and steadfast friends. He had revenged himself for what Bascom had done. He did not think a chief could build a life for his people based on hatred. He was at war because he had no other choice; it had been impossible to remain at peace.

He was just as determined as this man whom he called "older brother," to drive every foreigner out of their country. But this determination was a cool one, based on reason.

New soldiers came from the east, from Texas. These wore gray uniforms. They and the blue-coats fought, much to the Apaches' pleasure. The blue-coats withdrew, and for a time the gray-coats tried to control the Southwest. They, too, were few in numbers. They were less experienced in fighting Apaches than the blue-coats, and so even easier to get away from, or to trap and defeat.

There was an old trick that these new soldiers had to learn about. A small group of mounted Apaches would show themselves to a detachment of cavalry, exchange shots with them, perhaps, then turn and take flight. The detachment would come racing after them.

The Indians would stay in sight, but out of range. They would draw the soldiers into some narrow canyon, or a pass, or a steep valley, where other Apaches lay in ambush. The gray-coats were slow to learn about this, because sometimes there was not a single soldier left to tell about how his troop had been trapped.

The blue-coats returned, and there was more fighting. The men in gray retreated back into Texas. The others, the blue-coated enemies, took over the garrisons once more, but they were far too few. All the southern Apache tribes raided far and wide, as did the Navajos to the north.

The country of the southern Apaches took in more than half of New Mexico, a little less than half of Arizona, and a piece of Texas. You could mark it off by drawing a line on a map, east and west, a short distance south of Albuquerque, New Mexico.

Carry this line to the east across the Panhandle of Texas, to the west a little past the middle of Arizona. South of that, down to the Mexican border, was Apachería, except for a corner in the southwest part, where the Papago and Pima Indians lived. Over all that land, now, the tribes raged and raided.

North of that line in New Mexico was a sort of island of safety for White-Eyes, centering around the city of Santa Fe. There the Spanish-American population had established themselves strongly two hundred years earlier, and made allies of the Pueblo Indians who lived there. Many eastern Americans had settled there since the war with Mexico, so that there was a strong population, ready to defend itself.

Another Apache tribe, the Jicarillas, were friends with the Pueblo Indians and on fairly good terms with the white men. They had often joined in fighting the Plains tribes. They did not become allies of Cochise and Mangas Coloradas. But they, too, became restless and they made some trouble for the White-Eyes.

Neither did the Navajos, the greatest of all the Apache tribes, become allies. The Navajos, who lived west of the Santa Fe country, had customs different from the tribes of Cochise and Mangas. They even raised corn and beans, planted peach trees, wove blankets, and worked metal.

The Navajos did not particularly want to drive the white men out of the land. They found them useful. Those people, they said, raised sheep and horses and planted corn for the Navajos to take when they raided. If they wiped them out, or wiped out the Pueblos, then they, the Navajos, would have to do all that work! It was better to have them around handy and attack them from time to time.

It was fortunate for the Americans that these two tribes failed to join with Cochise and Mangas Colorados in those years when the Civil War had tied up the nation's strength. The large number of warriors they could have contributed would have made the fighting strength of the two sides more nearly even.

Then, too, the Utes, and perhaps some of the Pueblos might have joined in. The white men might really have been cleaned out of Arizona and New Mexico before the Civil War ended.

As it was, the struggle went on. At some of the army posts, if men went from one building to another at night, they walked with their pistols in their hands, and if they could, they went in groups. Apaches might be anywhere. About all the few soldiers could do was to defend their posts. It was almost a miracle when the mail came through to Tucson.

Then a change occurred. Mangas Coloradas had just sent word to Cochise to join him in an attack upon a mining settlement he was particularly anxious to get rid of. This was not to be a raid, but a full-scale attack with the intent of wiping out the place.

Just at this moment Cochise's scouts brought him a report of the largest body of blue-coated walking soldiers they had ever seen, moving towards the Chiricahua country from the west. They said that there were more than a thousand of these men, and some cavalry in addition. There were also, as usual, many wagons.

Two of these wagons were very strange. They seemed to consist of two pairs of wagons joined together. The first one was small. It had no cover, but two men rode on the top of it. Behind this was a two-wheeled wagon the body of which seemed to be a fat, black tube, not as long as a man.

Although the two wagons together did not seem to amount to much, the horses that pulled them acted as if they were heavy. The scouts guessed that the lead wagons might be full of that yellow metal the White-Eyes were so crazy about.

The matter of the wagons seemed unimportant. What concerned Cochise was the likelihood of a powerful attack upon his Stronghold. He sent Mangas an answering message, to the effect that he had all the fighting he could handle right there at home. In fact, if his older brother wanted a real battle, he might come and join the Chiricahuas.

More of Cochise's warriors had been killed

than there were new youths to replace them; at that time he had less than two hundred and fifty warriors. There might be no way in which he could avoid battle with the overwhelming force approaching him, and he could use a little help.

When Mangas got the message, he brought his fighting men to the Chiricahuas' mountain without delay. The two groups, combined, numbered about four hundred and fifty.

The soldiers were a regiment of California volunteers who had come to Arizona to clear out the Confederates. The Confederates were gone and the California volunteers turned their attention to the Apaches. The regiment's mission was to open the Pass for movements of troops between Arizona and New Mexico.

The soldiers came close to where trouble might be expected. They left their wagons behind, guarded by a company from another regiment and a troop of cavalry.

The army, as it seemed to the Apaches, wound its way into Apache Pass. The troops kept together, they scouted well, they gave every sign of being men of experience.

Cochise and Mangas watched them. Apache scouts moved about the flanks of the column. But the two chiefs did not dare attack. If the soldiers came against the Stronghold, the Apaches would stand and fight, but they could not possibly take the offensive.

On the second day, the scouts killed three soldiers who strayed away from the main body, but they could do no other damage. The regiment went on through, and camped out in the open, east of the mountains.

Cochise's scouts reported that now the wagons were moving. What had happened was that the commander of the regiment had sent word that he needed his supplies. Also, that it was important that the springs by the old Mail Station be held. So the captain in command set out on a forced march, planning to reach the springs, forty miles away.

This force was slightly smaller than that of the two Apache tribes. Clearly, the two Apache chiefs agreed, its coming offered a splendid chance to strike a hard blow at the enemy. There would be heavy fighting, but victory seemed almost certain.

As the two chiefs made their plans, Cochise, the born strategist, thought beyond the battle. If they could shatter the approaching troops they would, of course, capture the wagon

train, including those two strange wagons. He was curious about these. He knew how the blue-coats depended upon supplies. The capture of this train would make trouble for the army east of the mountains.

Then the army might send a detachment of its own back after fresh supplies, and there was the chance that that, too, could be defeated and that thus, little by little, the strength of that great force could be cut down. Running short of food, perhaps it would withdraw through the Pass, back to wherever it had come from. Perhaps, it would try an offensive action—would attack the Apaches here in their own mountains. With the Stronghold for a final stand, the chances for victory, even against double their numbers, were very good.

The plan for the coming battle was largely Cochise's. The enemy was making a long, tiring march. As the troops approached the springs, they would be tired and thirsty. The horses, after forty miles in the desert heat, would need water badly. The enemy, then, would try hard to get to the springs.

First they had to pass through a long, steep-sided valley. The ambush would be here. He and Mangas agreed that the soldiers would almost surely try to fight their way through to the second valley, where the springs were. The chiefs set their men to building stone breastworks commanding the water. Part of the force would be stationed around this valley, part around the first. In the end, the source of water would be a deathtrap.

It was always possible that the troops would fall back, and try to retreat the many miles to where water could be found. If they did, the Chiricahuas and Mimbrenos would keep them company all the way, and there would be many dead White-Eyes. The two chiefs did not think that the soldiers would try to camp without water. If they did, on the next day their horses would soon be useless.

Mangas and Cochise stationed half their men in each valley, with the thought that the soldiers would fight their way into the second, deeper part of the trap. They gave their subchiefs the necessary orders on what to do if the soldiers withdrew, if they went on into retreat, or if they camped.

CHAPTER XII

COCHISE LAY ON HIS STOMACH in the straggly grass on the ridge to the south of the first valley. His vision was fixed on the pass to the westward. His keen eyes made out thin swirls of dust that told that the troops were near. He studied the ridge on either side of him, and the north ridge, where Mangas and the Red Paint People lay. Most men would have said that there was not a living soul anywhere around. However, a trained Apache could make out, here and there, the motionless form of a warrior.

This would be the biggest fight Cochise had

ever had with the White-Eyes. It would do them more damage than any he had ever done, and it would be military damage, the most important of all. If this battle went as he had planned it, it would lead to a campaign with more hard, bloody fighting. Most likely, in the end, a clear-cut victory such as, up to then, neither side had ever won.

Once they had cut off that army to the east-ward, Mangas would call up the other Apache people against it. Perhaps once again, the blue-coats would be forced to withdraw from Apachería. He felt a little pulse of excitement in his stomach.

In the narrow slit between the mountains Cochise caught a glimmer of a blue figure, then another, then half a dozen. As he pressed himself yet closer to the ground, he breathed up a wordless prayer. Soon they would be here! Soon his plan would be tested.

*   *   *

The cavalry and wagons waited outside the valley. The infantry marched in, behind the fan of scouts. They seemed to move very slowly, as if the column would never all be in; but at last they were there. There were about twenty more of them than there were of the waiting Apaches. By the way the men moved and held themselves, Cochise could tell that they were tired. Still he waited. Not until the company was past the middle of the valley did he give the signal to open fire.

A storm of bullets and arrows fell upon the soldiers. They took cover, and fired in return, but all they could see to shoot at were the puffs of smoke from the Apaches' guns. After a short time, their commander gave orders to withdraw, and they moved back down the valley, firing as they retreated.

Some of the Apaches started to follow them, but Cochise and Mangas called them back. They had the taste of victory in their mouths, but they did not think the White-Eyes would give up as easily as that.

In a little while the troops came back. This time the cavalry was with them, so that they outnumbered the Indians in the first valley. Since the cavalry was there, the wagons also were brought along. Now, for the first time, Cochise got a good look at the strange wagons with the black tubes on them.

The blue-coats fought their way up the valley, and so into the larger, open space where the springs were. As they made for the water they so badly needed, they met a withering fire from the Apaches on the ridge, behind stone breastworks. Their advance was stopped.

The two chiefs brought the rest of their men up from the western valley to close the rear and stave off retreat. Cochise's heart was full of triumph. The enemy was surrounded and this time it was his people who had the greater strength!

The soldiers were doing something with those strange wagons. The horse pulling one of them, had been shot down. It had over-turned, and the men with it had been driven back by the Indians' fire. Now a number of them ran forward, righted the wagon with the tube, and dragged it back onto level ground. They were busy around the other one, too.

The men there made a good target; Cochise raised his rifle, aimed, and shot one. Then he turned his attention and his rifle elsewhere. At this stage of the battle, he would not waste bullets on men who were taking care of wagons. It was the men with rifles who had to be killed.

Suddenly there was a terrific roar, as loud as thunder. Flame spat from one of the tubes, followed by a great cloud of smoke. An enormous bullet struck the breastworks, knocking the edge down.

Cochise had time for the quick thought that these tubes were huge guns, and that they did not seem to be anything to worry about, and then the bullet exploded. Stones from the breastworks flew in all directions, carried, it seemed, by sheets of fire, and half a dozen Apaches lay scattered about, dead or wounded.

The second wagon-gun roared, and another shell exploded. Meanwhile, the first one was being reloaded. The chiefs as well as their people were terrified. They had never seen or heard of anything like this. They did not think that human beings could stand against those shells, which were more powerful than thunderbolts.

Surely, the White-Eyes had tamed thunder and lightning to their service! This was magic, terrible magic. Those warriors who were receiving the shellfire simply broke and ran; the others drew back in good order.

Cochise and Mangas consulted together. A few of their best warriors went singly to hiding places from which they could snipe at the enemy. One of them came back to report that eight of the cavalrymen were heading out of the valley to the westward, at a gallop.

In a way, that was good news. They were certainly messengers being sent to the forts beyond the San Pedro River. This meant that the soldiers' chief thought was that they needed help. Mangas immediately took a dozen of his warriors to chase them. Cochise remained in command of the main force, planning how he could renew the battle in spite of the wagon-guns.

Mangas and his men went after the messengers as fast as they could. After a few miles they came in sight of them, but they could not catch them. Both sides shot at each other from the saddle, but it is pure luck if a man, sitting on a running horse, hits his target. The Apaches did better at it than the White-Eyes. They killed a horse. Its rider jumped up behind another man. They killed a second and the same thing happened.

One rider's horse was somewhat slower than the others; he dropped behind. An Apache arrow hit the animal and it went down, but there was no one to pick up that soldier. He lay behind the body of his horse, rifle ready, to defend himself as best as he could.

Now Mangas made a curious mistake. He had set out to catch the messengers, to prevent them from bringing reinforcements. The sensible thing for him to do was to leave a couple of his men to watch the single soldier and keep on himself after the others. Instead, all the Apaches spread out in a half circle, and then began to move in upon the soldier.

This soldier's name was John Teal. He was a real fighter, and it happened that he had been issued one of the new, breech-loading rifles that were just beginning to come into use. As the Indians drew near, he fired. They, being used to muzzle-loaders, figured that then he would drop the rifle and draw his pistol. Instead, in a moment, he fired again, and then a third time.

Mangas and his men drew back. Here again was something unexpected and strange. This gun that went on shooting, coming right on top of the thunders of the wagon-guns, alarmed them. They saw this soldier would not be an easy kill. They circled about at some little distance from Teal.

Then Mangas moved in a little closer, to try a shot. Teal had already figured that this big man was some kind of a chief. He aimed carefully and fired, and Mangas toppled off his horse. The other Apaches rushed to him, picked him up, and galloped away.

As far as the Red Paint People were concerned, that ended the fight. When their chief was brought back to where his warriors were waiting, their only concern was to get help for him. They saw that he was seriously wounded. The whole body of them swooped down away from the battleground. Carrying Mangas as best they could, they traveled through the night as fast as they could go across country.

On the following day they entered a Mexican settlement in which lived a doctor of whom they had heard. The Mexicans were terrified when two hundred Apache braves, armed and painted for war, poured into their village.

The Indians took over the place, but they did no harm. They simply waited while the frightened doctor did what he could to save Mangas' life. Much to his relief, he was successful, for the Apaches had told him that if their chief died, he would die, too.

* * *

Cochise knew there was no use trying to hold the Red Paint People back after Mangas had been injured. He was left with his little band of Chiricahuas. He had thought he was about to taste victory; instead, he tasted the bitter ashes of defeat.

The next day, the column of blue-coated

soldiers formed and moved westward. A column on the march can suffer a good deal of damage from a quick attack, even if the attackers are fewer in numbers. The Chiricahuas made ready, taking positions along the line of march.

When Cochise thought the time was ripe, he gave his orders, and the warriors showed themselves. Very quickly the wagon-guns were unlimbered and two shells burst among them. That was enough; the warriors fell back.

The soldiers went on to join the main force to the east. Then, shortly, more came to the springs, a strong body, with wagon-guns.

There they built a fort. This was a real fort, not just a collection of buildings like Fort Buchanan. High, strong walls surrounded it, and wagon-guns were placed along the walls. The garrison that was left there was almost as large as the whole force of the Chiricahuas.

There was nothing Cochise could do about it. He could still make Apache Pass unsafe for small parties of travelers, but with the fort in the heart of his country, and always more soldiers to the east and west, he could not stop troops from moving through as they might choose.

CHAPTER XIII

THE APACHE WAR CONTINUED. That other, greater war in the East drew to a close. Lee surrendered the Army of Virginia. One by one the lesser Southern generals gave up the hopeless struggle. More blue-coated troops came to the Southwest. It looked as if nobody could win, as if the sniping, the raiding, the killing would go on forever.

At that time there was a man in Tucson named Thomas J. Jeffords. Captain Jeffords (as he was sometimes called) had been in Arizona for five or six years, and during that time had become an expert Indian fighter.

Unlike most Americans in that part of the country, he had taken a good deal of trouble to learn about the Apaches. He even spoke their language moderately well.

Jeffords had just given up his contract to carry the United States mail between Tucson and the East. Despite the fort in Apache Pass, despite the increased number of soldiers round about, getting the mail through seemed nearly hopeless. In the sixteen months that he had the contract, the Chiricahuas had killed fourteen of his men, and he himself had had some very narrow escapes.

He had decided to take up prospecting, instead. In the course of his scouting, and from conversations he had had with Indians, he thought he knew some likely places to look for gold. Prospecting in the Southwest was extremely dangerous, for a lone man or a small party. Worse, Jeffords wanted to work fairly close to the Chiricahuas' home country.

He formed a plan which, if they had known about it, would have made any other white men sure that he was crazy. He decided to go visit Cochise and make a private peace with him. He had made a point of gathering information about the chief, separating out the truth from among the mass of lies and wild rumors. He believed that if he could win Cochise's trust, he could depend on the chief's word completely.

To carry out his plan he needed help from an Apache. There generally were a few "friendly" Apaches living around the larger settlements such as Tucson. Some of these were men who found the white man's way of life—working for money, buying the white man's food—easier than the Apache's work of hunting and fighting. Some were in trouble with their own people. Some were friendly only for as long as suited them to trade with the white men. Some were spies.

One such Indian was a friend of Jeffords. This Indian was startled when he learned of Jeffords' plan, but after some talk he agreed to it. Without telling anyone else, the two men set out together for the Chiricahua country.

Cochise himself did not ordinarily go out on raids, since the war had started. He had raiding parties out in all directions. It was his duty to stay at the center, to control everything, and to spend much time thinking for his people. He was occupied in this way when Jeffords came into the Chiricahua country.

Cochise was thinking wearily that he saw no

end to this war, and certainly no hope of victory. The Mescaleros and the Navajos had been conquered and put on reservations. The Jicarillas, he heard, had made peace. He did not care about the Jicarillas or the Navajos, but the Mescaleros were old allies. Their surrender was a real loss to himself and Mangas.

His young men were happy with a life of constant warfare and the taking of much booty, but he and the old men, his counsellors, saw that each year there were a few less men of fighting age. There were many children. Each year strong youths completed their training; and nowadays the novices quickly served their four war parties, and became warriors. Still, the numbers grew less, even though only by a few.

During those years of peace Cochise had seen his people growing stronger year by year, and his heart had been good because of that. In those years they had raided into Mexico when and as they chose. There had been no other fighting; not many were killed. There had been just fighting enough to keep the warriors in training and to ensure a fair amount of booty. They had been good days.

He let his thoughts wander to the madness

of the child chief. He considered again the curious fact, like a bad joke, that such a man should have made a war. Then he turned his thoughts away from all that, not to waste his strength on things that could not be changed, or on anger or grief. A good many of his warriors were idle at the moment. He began studying on a plan for spoiling the sleep of the soldiers at the fort.

He was interrupted by a scout who brought him strange news. A smoke signal in the west said that a lone White-Eyes was coming in peace. Cochise told the scout to pick up a few more young men and to investigate.

When the warrior had gone, the chief meditated on what the white man might want. He could hardly believe that a single American would visit the Chiricahuas, for any purpose.

He rose and went among his people, and arranged for a second group of scouts to see that there were no soldiers coming along behind this man. He arranged for careful scouting in all directions, to make sure that this was not a new and especially clever trap.

Further reports came in. The man was truly alone. He was not a blue-coat, but he was well armed. One of the scouts remembered seeing this man when he took part in an attack on the mail, and that he had fought well and skillfully. The white man had come part way with an Apache who wore an American hat and trousers. It was this Apache who made the smoke signal.

Later, a scout came in, who had talked with the Apache. This scout had investigated the reason for the coming of the white man. The Apache said that the White-Eyes wanted to speak to Cochise himself. The American was alone now. The Apache had turned back and had ridden away towards Tucson.

There was no sign of a trap in any direction; no troops were moving. As the news came in, Cochise's wonder grew. His first impulse had been to refuse to see the White-Eyes unless it should be to watch him being killed. His curiosity made him change his mind. The chief gave orders that the man be watched closely, but not harmed.

Late the next day, Jeffords rode into the Chiricahuas' camp and dismounted. Every Indian who could manage it was on hand. They stood or sat in a wide circle, studying the stranger and not speaking.

Cochise, standing behind the circle, looked the White-Eyes over. He saw a big man, arrayed in Western style, with fair, rather long hair, and a reddish-blond beard. The man had the light-colored eyes from which came the Apache name for Americans. He had a six-shooter hanging from his belt, a knife, and a rifle on his saddle.

Cochise stepped forward. Jeffords recognized him immediately. His unusual height would have been enough, but his face, too, proclaimed him the chief. Jeffords took off his belt and pistol and handed them to Cochise. Then he handed over his rifle and

his knife. "Let your women take care of these for me while we talk," he said.

Cochise signalled to his wife, who came to him and took the weapons. He told a young man to take care of the horse. Then, to Jeffords, he said simply, "Come," and turned away.

Jeffords followed him as the Chiricahuas moved aside, leaving a passage. Jeffords saw that all their eyes were on him. He could tell nothing of their thoughts. His heart was pounding, but he kept his face calm and walked as if he were completely at ease.

Cochise led him to his shelter, and signed to him to sit. They sat in silence for a minute or so. Cochise was as curious as his visitor was excited. But he showed an indifferent expression, as if he hardly knew that anyone was there.

He accepted the tobacco and papers Jeffords offered. Both of the men made and lit cigarettes. Cochise still waited. This man wanted something, let him speak first. Already the chief was beginning to like this stranger because he was calm and unafraid, because there was a straightness, a decency in his eyes.

At length Jeffords spoke. "For a long time I have been fighting you. Until a month ago,

I was chief over the mail. Your people killed many of my men. Several times they nearly killed me. Now I have stopped that work. I do not like work in which I am obliged to send men to be killed. I do not like carrying talking papers for people who would be afraid to carry them themselves."

Cochise smoked and listened, his face blank. He liked the way this man talked.

Jeffords went on. He had thought a long time about what he would say. "I have been thinking about looking for the yellow metal, which I can use to trade with my people. Then I thought, what is the good of going out and looking for that, what is the good of finding it, if the Chiricahuas find me? I thought that the only way would be to make peace with your people, so I have come to see you."

Cochise let a little more time go by. "My young men have told me that you had to do with the mail," he answered. "They told me that you fight well. There are one or two less of them because of you, I think."

Jeffords wisely kept silent.

Cochise went on. "This idea of making peace with just one man—I shall think about it. You ask for peace, but you have shown that you are not afraid. You have been willing to trust your life in my hands. I say, I shall think about it. I think now that the women have food ready for us."

They ate together. Through the evening they talked of many things. Steadily Cochise's liking for the younger man grew stronger. The belief grew upon him that here was someone like Steen, the soldier chief with whom he had made peace. Here was a man to trust.

He found an unexpected satisfaction in telling someone, on the other side, his story of the trouble with the child chief and the business of the stolen Miguel, a boy he had never heard of. As he went on in life, he thought more and more deeply about the ways of Yusn, about religion. He was curious to know what a White-Eyes thought on that subject. They talked long into the night.

Jeffords was a frontiersman. He was fairly well educated, and he had led a rough hard life. He had enough vision to be impressed by the Chiricahua chief, just as deeply as the chief was by him. He had thought he might find nobility and honor in the man, but he was finding much more than that. To his surprise, he felt ever greater liking for him as their talk went on.

The next day Cochise put his hand on the white man's shoulder. This was unusual in itself, for the chief did not usually like to touch people or be touched by them. He said, "I shall give you what you ask. There will be peace between you and the Chiricahuas. You may move through our country as you will, and you will always be welcome here. From now on, I look upon you as my nephew."

Jeffords did not hurry back to Tucson. By the time he left the Chiricahua settlement, he and Cochise were firmly and permanently friends. Later, it was to be Jeffords' lot on a few occasions to guide troops against the Apaches, but the Chiricahuas understood that such things had to be done. It did not break the friendship, nor end the white man's freedom to go and come through the Indians' country.

When he went, Cochise was sorry to see him go. In the following days, as the chief went on with the business of war and the governing of his tribe, he also thought of his new "nephew" with pleasure. There was something about him that made the chief feel happy.

CHAPTER XIV

TWO MORE YEARS OF WAR went by. Everywhere the Apaches were losing. Where once four thousand warriors had fought and raided from the southern edges of Utah and Colorado to the Mexican border, only the Chiricahuas remained in the field as an unbroken tribe. Fragments of other tribes still roamed free, sometimes attacking, often hunted. But the greater part of the Apache people were now on reservations, disarmed and guarded by troops.

Cochise, with a force that was hardly larger than an infantry company, held the Chiricahua country still inviolate. More, he carried the war constantly to the enemy, raiding far and wide. That raiding was one of the secrets of his success. Citizens everywhere clamored for troops to be stationed near them to protect them. As a result, the United States forces were scattered, trying to be ready at all the places where the Chiricahuas might strike.

One autumn day in 1870, Jeffords rode into Cochise's camp in the Stronghold. He had been busy, and had not visited there in many months. Today he rode with a purpose, another of those surprising ideas of his.

Cochise was glad to see him. Now that their friendship was firmly established, the Indian did not expect his nephew to explain why he was there. He might be visiting just out of friendliness, he might just have been passing by. If he had business, he would tell about it when he got ready, in the evening, after they had eaten, or the next day, when he was rested.

In fact, the bearded man did not speak of what was on his mind until well along in the following morning, when he found himself alone with the chief. On the evening of his arrival, several Chiricahuas had dropped in at Cochise's camp. They too, had come to like the White-Eyes whom one could treat as a friend. They liked to listen to his news of the great world, far beyond the limits of the lands they knew.

It was Jeffords who had first given some ideas of the nature and size of the Civil War. On this visit he brought news of a war that had broken out on the other side of the ocean, between the French and the Germans.

These older men, sub-chiefs, who were free to gather by Cochise's fire, were impressed and disturbed, as they grasped some idea of how many White-Eyes there were in the world. The numbers Jeffords spoke of were so large that they were puzzled how to put the words into the Apache speech. Jeffords encouraged this line of thought; it suited his purpose.

The next morning, when the sun was high, Jeffords and Cochise sat together under an oak tree, on a rise of ground looking out through one of the entrances to the Stronghold. The entrance was a narrow way between two cliffs, which was partly closed by a rough wall of stone. The sun struck the north wall, lighting up the warm-colored stone until it glinted and glimmered as if it had gold in it.

The end of the gap framed a view of a

green ridge a mile or so away. Beyond that was the purplish mass of a distant, high mountain top.

Cochise said, "I can say that there are about three thousand of my people, a little less than that, men, women, and children. I have those words and I know what they mean. Last night, when we talked of your people and of those white-eyed people across the water, we had to make up ways of saying how many there were. And even then, we were speaking only of the fighting men.

"I have been trying to understand that many people. I have been trying to understand all the others that there must be behind them, the women, and the ones too old or too young for the warpath."

He paused, picked up a pinch of the dry, sandy earth, and let it fall. "It is like the sand in the dry places down below the mountains, I think. If you rode all day counting the sand as far as you could see, the sand would all be White-Eyes. And then you would get off your horse and in one corner you would find this." He scooped up a handful of the earth and looked at it. "This is the Chiricahuas."

He did not let the sand fall from his palm.

He studied it a moment. He had said, "This is the Chiricahuas." Having said that, he must be careful, lest through this handful of dirt he did a harm to his people. He put it back carefully in its place.

This was the lead Jeffords wanted. It was a miracle that Cochise had given him so good an opening. "That is true. And with your little handful you have been fighting all of those for ten years. For the last few years the Chiricahuas have been fighting almost alone. The Chiricahuas can be proud. But how long can you go on?"

Cochise said, "I do not know."

"How many warriors do you count now?" Jeffords pressed the point.

"Two hundred and nineteen. This last month we lost five. We have two novices out now serving war parties, and there are three who will be ready soon." Day by day Cochise counted the strength of his people. He did not hesitate to give the figures to Jeffords; he knew that what he said would never be repeated to the enemy.

"Always a few less." Jeffords paused. "Always the fighting. As you well know, even I have had to guide war parties coming

against your people. I have done that twice this past year."

"I know. And if, when you are working against us, one of my young men should kill you, he would be much honored. We know that you are a clever scout, a dangerous warrior." A hint of a smile showed at the corners of Cochise's mouth as he spoke. This was unusual for him. Most Apaches love a joke and laugh readily, but Cochise seldom smiled and almost never laughed.

Jeffords said, "A man must be willing to be killed, or live like a woman. Still, I am in no hurry to die. I wish this war could be ended."

"You know how it started," Cochise answered. "I wanted peace. I still want peace. It was not my doing. You know that story."

"Yet, if the war goes on, you will grow weaker and weaker. If I am killed, if I kill one of your young men, that is that. But what happens if one day there are no more Chiricahuas? What then?"

Cochise made a gesture with his open hand, letting it fall forward, palm up. "Perhaps that is how it must end. Who knows Yusn's will?"

"Would it not be better to make peace now, while you are still strong?"

Cochise waited before he answered. For an instant, he grew suspicious of his friend, his adopted nephew. Could this man, too, be a traitor? Then the suspicion left him. He knew Jeffords spoke honorably.

"With whom shall I make peace? I can make peace with you, one single man, because you have honor. But to make peace with all your people—who is there who has honor?"

Jeffords said, doubtfully, "The Indian Agent. . ."

The chief interrupted him with a sweep of his hand. "He will not even protect the ones who have surrendered. He is no chief. He has no power! I have heard of these agents, one in Tucson and one in Santa Fé. They write talking papers, and steal the food that is sent for the Apaches who have been made prisoners."

Jeffords did not answer.

"You know what happened to the Arivaipas a few months ago. I do not have to tell you that, I think." Cochise's voice had become hard as he talked.

"I know."

They were silent for some little time. Cochise was arranging his thoughts, seeking calmness. Jeffords was remembering the Arivaipa Apaches.

After many defeats, the greater part of that tribe had given up to the Army. They were placed on a piece of land a few miles from Tucson, under guard of a detail of soldiers. There, at the request of their chief, men had been sent to show them how to farm and they had planted some gardens.

The presence of these Apaches so near the town caused a turmoil in Tucson. The boasters, who killed Indians by the hundreds in their talk but who had never faced a rifle, grew angrier and angrier. The talk of how the only good Apache was a dead one became strong.

This anger was fanned by a group of clever men who became known in history as the Tucson Ring. They were business men, men of property. They did not want peace, because they were making great profits out of war. They sold supplies to the Army at high prices, and in secret they sold arms and ammunition to the Apaches, also at high prices. If the wars ended, these propertied citizens would lose money.

It did not suit them to see the Arivaipas established in peace. They were afraid that the sight of them would lead too many others to come in and give themselves up. These men worked on the mob, building up hatred.

A small band of Chiricahuas made a raid across the San Pedro. At that moment, the only troops on hand who could be used to turn back the raid were the ones guarding the Arivaipas, so they were ordered to do so. The Arivaipas were left unguarded. It happened also that at that time most of the men of the tribe had permission to hunt, and had gone into the mountains.

In Tucson the mob formed, guided secretly by the Ring. The mob invited a number of Papago Indians to join them. The Papagos, famous for their skill with war clubs, were deadly enemies of the Apaches. The mob of white Americans, Mexicans, and Papagos, stole into the peaceful settlement of the Apaches before dawn. They went from hut to hut, murdering the sleeping Indians with clubs.

Finally, a woman woke and screamed. The others woke. A few men tried hopelessly to fight, the rest took flight.

The mob turned to using its guns, hunting down all they could find. They killed eighty-nine Arivaipas, only ten of whom were men, and took back to Tucson with them twenty-nine children. They intended to take the children into Mexico and sell them as slaves. Jeffords remembered how the town of Tucson had celebrated this massacre as a great victory.

At length Cochise said, "Has anyone been punished for that business?"

"No," Jeffords answered. "Some were arrested, but they have been turned loose."

"You see." The chief spoke quietly, thoughtfully. It was good to put into words, in talking with his nephew, things he had been thinking over for so long. "We have seen, we have known, that when Apaches make peace, they are put on some poor piece of dry land that nobody wants. There the soldiers guard them, the Agent cheats them, and they starve slowly."

Jeffords was silent and Cochise continued, "They sit, they cannot make their livings. They cease to be men, I think. But there is worse than that. If they come in to make peace, the soldiers may just kill them, then and there. And if the soldiers do not kill them, then your people who are not soldiers will come and do it. What sort of peace is this?"

Jeffords still had nothing to say.

"You know what happened to me under the white flag," Cochise said. "A year ago my teacher, my elder brother, that one who used to be chief of the Red Paint People—he went to the soldiers to make peace. He went with a white flag. He was not a warrior any longer; he was seventy years old. He went to one of your soldier chiefs, with his white flag, and told him he had come to make peace. That night they cut him to death with bayonets.

"It would be better even for an old man to die on the warpath, while he was making his living, I think."

Jeffords picked up a small stick and scratched idly in the dirt with it. Cochise paused a moment, to regain his calm. He kept his voice quiet and thoughtful.

"The soldiers showed a white flag to the Pinaleños. We do not like the Pinaleños too well, but hear what happened to them. Some soldier chiefs stood by the white flag to talk peace. The soldiers lay hidden all around. The Pinaleños came to the flag. Some of their women came with them. Then the officers stepped back and the soldiers started shooting. Very many were killed that day. They have peace, you may say."

Jeffords said, painfully, "I have heard."

"With whom can I make peace?" Cochise asked. "Listen to me. Yusn is over us all. He is over us, and around us, and in us. Different peoples think of Yusn differently. That is because no one can really know him, I think. We can only try to come near him, to bring him into ourselves. There are men among your people who think about Yusn, they say. They say there are men among you who seek him. You are one, although you are still young. You will seek him more when you are older. But where are the others?"

Cochise took time again to think, then he went on. "Your chiefs cannot be trusted. They lie. They cheat. For that reason, I think, your people do not listen to the men who seek for Yusn. Your great chief in Washington, does he try to fill himself with Yusn? Does he pray? No, I think.

"For more than ten years the chiefs he has sent out here have been liars; by that I must measure him. Bad men can be kept from doing harm only when a strong, good chief is over them to punish them. My nephew, show me such a chief among your people. Show me a true chief into whose heart I can look, and who can look into mine. Show me a chief who can keep the thieves and liars from following their natures, and I will make peace with him. Do you know such a chief?"

Jefferds said, "No. Not here. But the President—the great chief in Washington—I know that he is a good man. He is so far from here, I think he does not know how things are here."

"Can you go and tell him?"

"No. I am too small."

"You see, there is nothing for us to do but fight. If we all die, we die here, in the land we love, and we die free. We do not die slowly of hunger and hopelessness. We do not die by being murdered when we sleep." He looked out through the gap, he looked around at the cliffs, the trees, the mountains, with great love in his eyes. "That way I am willing to die. And that is how it is with all my people."

Jeffords said, "My friend, my uncle, I hear you. I came here hoping we could find a way out of this war, but as I listen to you my heart says 'yes.' "

CHAPTER XV

IN THE ELEVENTH YEAR OF the Chiricahuas' war the fort still stood in Apache Pass. Other forts ringed the Chiricahua country. Scattered fragments of other Apache tribes remained free and still made raids. From time to time, desperate and forced by hunger, a few warriors on the reservations made bows or dug up hidden weapons and slipped out on the warpath. All of these together amounted to but little.

The troops in New Mexico and Arizona were no longer companies, nor were they only regiments commanded by colonels. They were small armies.

At various times foreign troops fought their way deep into the Chiricahua country; they even tried to attack the Stronghold. Always, they were driven back. They never even reached the Stronghold itself. The passes that led to it were steep and narrow. A few determined and brave men could hold them even against armies.

In that year, against those odds, Cochise and his warriors made fifty-four attacks against their enemy, and in these attacks they killed forty-seven White-Eyes. They captured many of the new, breech-loading rifles. They fed well on the animals they ran off.

By then, almost all the Coyotero Apaches had been put on their reservation. In August, there were five of these—young men, who got so restless that they simply could not stand it. They felt as if their lives were seeping away in idleness. All their days were spent sitting around doing nothing. They made up their minds to slip off the reservation and have a war party.

Their original plan was to go on foot, secretly, until they reached Mexico. Over the border, they could steal or capture horses, and then start really raiding. This plan meant that they would have to walk nearly two hundred miles, but they were ready for that.

One of these young men had a musket hidden in the cliffs, along with several bullets and enough gunpowder for two or three shots. Three of them went to work in hiding, making bows and arrows. The last spent three weeks and a great deal of planning to steal a loaded pistol from one of the officers of the troops that guarded them. At the end of the third week, in the beginning of September, he succeeded.

One night the five of them slipped out of the Indians' camp, one by one. They met where the Salt River falls over red rocks. As they traveled from there, they took care to step on rocks, on hard trampled earth, on anything that would not leave tracks. When they walked on sandy ground, they took leafy branches and brushed their tracks over as they went.

From time to time the troops were accustomed to hold a roll call to make sure that all the Coyoteros were on hand. They did not do this regularly. If the five had stuck to their scheme, they would have been nearly at the

Mexican border before their absence was noticed.

On the second day, however, they passed an irrigated ranch at which nobody was home. There was a whole string of good horses in a fenced pasture. That was too much for the Apaches. They took one apiece and rode off. When the rancher returned, he found his property missing. Scouting around, he found a moccasin track. He reported right away to the commanding officer on the reservation. The officer held a roll call, and sent out an alarm for the five runaways.

A detail of cavalry was ordered up from the south to try to cut them off. Jeffords was employed to go with this detail as scout. He was willing to do such work when it had nothing to do with Chiricahuas. Also, he liked Captain Holmes, who commanded the detail.

When they had been out a week, without having any luck at all, the party camped about fifty miles northwest of the edge of the Chiricahua country. There was here an open valley in which was a good spring, grass for the horses, and a number of trees. Captain Holmes thought it a good place to rest his command.

Jeffords rode out to scout alone while the

soldiers took it easy. In a canyon he found the tracks of two horses that clearly were being ridden. The tracks were not scattered around from one clump of straggly grass to another, as the tracks of loose horses would have been.

Jeffords was pretty sure that the horses which had made the tracks belonged to Chiricahuas. The Chiricahuas often put a buckskin cap on their horses' hooves to protect them in travel through sand or over rock. The tracks showed that these horses were shod in that manner.

Jeffords decided to try to find the two riders. He thought they might be able to give him word of the Coyoteros. Also, he did not want to be forced to help the soldiers chase Chiricahua warriors.

The tracks were clear in the sand, so that for a mile or so he could follow them at a brisk trot. Then he came to a grassy place. He lost the tracks. He got off his horse to look more closely. While he was studying the ground, a voice behind him said in Apache, "Have you lost something, my cousin?"

He turned around to see a young man, Pontsay, standing and watching him. Pontsay was Mangas Coloradas' nephew. After his

uncle was murdered and his tribe surrendered, he had brought his wife and child and joined the Chiricahuas.

Jeffords raised his hand in greeting. Pontsay's face was guarded. He carried his rifle in the crook of his left arm, and his right hand lightly grasped the stock by the hammer. His forefinger was not far from the trigger.

"Are you scouting for Chiricahuas?" Pontsay asked.

"No. I am scouting for Coyoteros. But I seemed to see the tracks of some friends, and I thought it would be well if they stayed away from those soldiers."

Pontsay's right hand fell from the trigger and he smiled. "Good. They will not see us."

"Who is with you?" Jeffords asked.

"Your little brother." Pontsay meant Chee, who was Cochise's nephew.

"I'd like to see Chee and talk with you both," Jeffords said, "but I think it better not to stay over this way too long. Have you seen any sign of Coyoteros?"

"No sign," Pontsay said.

"Well, then there are no Apaches over this way at all, so tomorrow the blue-coats will be led farther west."

Pontsay smiled again. "That's right. You

only dreamed about meeting your friends." Then he added, "If you want to eat broiled rabbit, up this branch here, there is a clump of willows and a little water. You might find some rabbit there this evening."

Jeffords rejected the invitation. "There wouldn't be enough to go round if the soldiers got curious and came after me. Speak to Chee for me. Tell my uncle I am well. May we both live well and meet again."

"May we both live well," the warrior answered.

Jeffords mounted and rode back towards the camp. He was sorry not to go to the Apaches' hiding place and see Chee. Chee had something of his uncle's nobility, and in addition, he was lively and had a good sense of fun.

As Jeffords rode towards the tents of the camp, he saw a troop of cavalry coming from the south. At the head of it rode a tall man, with white hair and a flowing, white beard. He wore the uniform and insignia of a general. Jeffords recognized the impressive figure of General O. O. Howard, the highest ranking officer ever to visit Arizona.

People thought that General Howard was slightly queer. He was intensely pious. He always carried his Bible with him. He read from it every day, and guided all his actions by its teachings. To most soldiers, as well as the rough men of the frontier, such behavior was truly strange. And still, they knew that he was a good soldier, well proven in battle. They did not know quite what to make of him.

General Howard had been sent out by the President to try to settle the Apache problem. That meant, Jeffords thought, to settle the Chiricahua problem. He wondered if the old man thought he could pray them into surrendering. He'd have a tough time doing that. The Chiricahuas were pretty powerful at praying themselves.

Jeffords rode into camp, turned his horse over to a soldier, and went into his tent. He was rather tired. He settled himself in his camp chair and drowsed. Faintly he heard the sounds of the cavalry troop arriving, the order "Present arms!" as the general came near, and then voices outside his own tent. His eyelids closed more heavily. A voice at the door of his tent said, "Mr. Jeffords, may I come in?"

Jeffords opened his eyes. Then his head jerked up, and he rose to his feet. General

Howard paused, then came into the tent.

"Pardon my breaking in on you like this, sir," the general said. "I have ridden here specially to find you."

There was a quiet authority in General Howard's manner, but he was unusually polite and mild for so high an officer.

Jeffords said, "General, I am honored. Won't you sit down?" He pointed to his chair.

The general said, "I would not take your only chair, sir."

"Please do," Jeffords answered. "I am well used to sitting on the ground."

"I have been a soldier all my life. I am used to that, too. Sit down, please." As he said this, the general lowered himself to the ground and made himself comfortable, sitting cross-legged. Jeffords took the chair. Already he realized that this man was unlike anyone he had ever known. The general said, "I have heard of your friendship with Cochise. What kind of a man is he?"

Jeffords thought carefully before he answered. "He is a fighter. When he hates, he hates with all his being. At times, he is a cruel savage. But he is a warm and true friend."

Jeffords saw that Howard was listening closely to every word. "Cochise is the real thing in chiefs; he is wise, and he thinks always of his people. He is a man of honor. He always keeps his word; he never breaks a promise. For that reason, he has no use whatever for anyone who tells a lie, or fails to keep a promise."

Jeffords hesitated, then added, "He is deeply pious. He gives a good deal of his time to prayer and to thinking about his religion."

Howard was silent for a moment. Then he said, "That is certainly a different picture from what most men out here give me."

"It is the true one," Jeffords replied.

Howard said, "I talked to Colonel Steen before I came out. It was he who made the peace with Cochise. He gave much the same picture, except that he did not speak about Cochise's religion. You seem to know the man more closely than Steen did."

"Most likely." Jeffords thought of the long days he had spent, warmed by Cochise's friendship.

"As you may know, I have been sent out by the President of the United States." General Howard spoke briskly now. "I have full authority to make any settlement I think right."

Jeffords nodded.

The general studied his face for a moment, then he said, "Mr. Jeffords, will you take me to see Cochise?"

It took Jeffords a little time to realize what the general had asked. "You want to meet Cochise?"

"Yes," said the general. "How else can I make peace?"

Jeffords thought, at last the right man comes to Arizona. Right away he decides to do the one, simple, straightforward thing that no one had thought of in eleven years of bloody war.

"Are you willing to go without an escort?" he asked.

"Yes, if you think that is the way to do."

"It is the only way." Jeffords meditated briefly. "Of course, you go as one great chief visiting another. I think you can take your aide and a striker or so."

"Very well," Howard agreed. "When can you arrange this?"

"Right away," said Jeffords. "I must have a fresh horse, and will you please see that no one attempts to follow me? By great good luck, I know where I can find the chief's nephew. I'll be back before dark."

The general rose. "Good. It will be done as you ask."

They left the tent together.

*   *   *

As Jeffords rode up to the clump of willows, Chee stepped forward out of hiding. "Elder brother," he said.

"Younger brother," Jeffords replied in greeting.

Chee smiled. "Is the White-Eyes' food so bad that you had to come looking for rabbit after all?"

Jeffords did not reply in joking fashion. "I come with news of a great thing," he said.

"Come in and tell us," replied Chee, immediately serious.

Jeffords dismounted and followed Chee to where Pontsay sat by a small, smokeless fire. The white man explained what had happened, and told his impression of General Howard.

Finally he said, "Send word to my uncle that this is the man, I think. He is a man of prayer. He lives in harmony with Yusn."

Chee said gravely, "We shall tell him." Then his smile appeared again at the corners of his mouth. "But, my big brother, we two are poor men. We came out this way to earn our living. We were going to see if we could find a horse or two. Now you ask us to go home emptyhanded. Our wives will scold us."

Jeffords said, "Would it make you unhappy if the soldier-chief made you a present of a horse?"

"I would not cry," Chee answered, and smiled again when Jeffords said he thought this could be arranged.

They planned a meeting at the mouth of a canyon to the southward for the next morning. Then Jeffords rode back to camp.

He reported in detail to General Howard. They talked together until after dark. When the scout rolled up in his blankets, he did not fall asleep right away. He felt a new excitement. Perhaps this really was the man! Perhaps now the war, so needlessly unleashed, would be ended. Perhaps the Chiricahuas would be saved, and the chief he so loved could spend his old age in peace.

He did not know. There was so much that could go wrong. Howard was a truly good man, that was clear. But would he give the Chiricahuas the terms they had to have? How could he ensure their safety? It was all perhaps, perhaps. He fell asleep with that word in his mind.

CHAPTER XVI

JEFFORDS AND GENERAL HOWARD set out early the next morning. They were accompanied by Captain Sladen, Howard's aide, and two enlisted men.

Captain Holmes and the other officers had not wanted to let the general go among the Chiricahuas without a strong escort. They were afraid for him, and they knew that if he were killed, they might be held responsible. They thought, too, of the uproar there would be if Cochise decided to hold a famous major-general as a hostage. The general had stood firm, and overruled their protests.

At the mouth of the canyon Howard's party met the two Apaches. When Jeffords introduced them, Chee and Pontsay greeted the general in Spanish and offered their hands, as they had seen the white men do. General Howard looked at them pleasantly, took their hands, and said *"Buenos días,"* which was all the Spanish he knew.

Captain Sladen met the Apache warriors in the same manner. The enlisted men stared. They knew why they were there; they knew what the general planned. Even so, the sight of these officers and Mr. Jeffords talking peacefully with two painted, half-naked Apache devils amazed them.

General Howard presented the Indians with a horse. The party traveled all day. As they went along, the Indians studied the general. In the late afternoon Chee told Jeffords, "Perhaps you are right. Perhaps this is the man our uncle can talk with."

They were in the foothills of the Chiricahua Mountains when they made camp by a spring. Chee slipped away to talk to the scouts who had been trailing them for the last few hours. When he came back his wife was with him. Several other families joined the camp at sunset, and so did four of the scouts.

Howard noted with interest how these warriors seemed to appear out of nowhere. The two enlisted men noted it, too. It made them uneasy, but the general was perfectly calm and confident. After supper, he read a little in his Bible by the light of the fire. Then he got up, walked a short distance from the camp, and knelt to pray. He knew that many eyes were watching him in the starlight, but that did not disturb him. Both Chee and Pontsay were deeply impressed.

In the morning a messenger came from Cochise. He told Jeffords that the chief thought there were too many in the party. He understood that the soldier-chief would want to have his counsellor with him. He supposed that that was what the other officer was for. But he did not think the White-Eyes needed the two soldiers. It occurred to Jeffords that Cochise might be testing the general.

He explained the matter to Howard, who ordered the men to return to headquarters. Half a dozen warriors mounted to escort the returning soldiers. This was necessary, as there were war parties out. The soldiers rode off, amazed and uneasy all over again.

Howard and those with him traveled a second day, ever higher into the mountains, and camped again. In the middle of the third morning they came to the Stronghold.

The general studied the approaches with interest. He saw that it was as he had been told, a place where a few, determined men could stand off even a powerful force. A company of good troops, he thought, could hold out here against a brigade.

There was a wide, level space inside, behind the cliffs. In the middle there was a good spring and a swampy area. The grass was good. There was room to graze a good many horses and cattle. Howard saw that the defenders of this place could keep fighting for a long time without running out of food or water.

Most of the Chiricahua women and children and many of the men were gathered in a wide circle. Some of them were standing, others were seated. The party rode into this circle and dismounted. Several boys who were novice warriors came to take their horses.

An unusually big, heavy-set Apache came to greet Jeffords. Jeffords introduced him as one of Cochise's sons. Then there was a stir in the crowd. Talk stopped. A tall, straight man, nearly sixty years old, came toward General Howard.

Jeffords said, "This is the chief." He did not need to say it. The general knew that as soon as he saw the man's face.

Cochise did as his nephew had done. He held out his hand in the white man's way and said, *"Buenos días."* The two men studied each other. Jeffords, watching them, thought that here indeed were two chiefs. Here were two great men.

Cochise led the way to a comfortable spot by a clump of bushes, where they could sit or lie on the grass and talk in quiet. Jeffords interpreted; Captain Sladen listened.

Cochise began at the beginning, as Indians like to do. He told about Major Steen and the peace they had made together. He told how he had protected the travelers in the Pass against other Apache tribes. He told how once he had put several Chiricahuas to death for attacking a stagecoach. Then he came to the story of Bascom and the white flag.

As he described those events Howard saw the chief's face darken and grow harsh. The general saw the other side of Cochise; he saw the man who could hate; he saw the killer.

Howard knew all these things that Cochise recounted, but he listened patiently. When Cochise paused, he said, "I have heard that story. Tell him that in my opinion Bascom disgraced the uniform he wore. Tell him that I would never permit such a man to serve under my command."

When Jeffords interpreted that, Cochise's expression lightened. He went on with his story. The Chiricahua chief was serving several purposes in going over the whole history of his war. He was relieving his feelings. He was making sure that this soldier-chief understood exactly what the situation of his people was.

Also, as he talked, he watched. He studied the general's face. He saw just how the man reacted to each thing said. In this way he was learning a good deal about the American. So now Cochise talked about how Mangas was murdered. He spoke of the massacres of the Pinaleños and the Arivaipas. He talked about what happened to the Apaches who had gone onto reservations.

This was Cochise's day. All through it he talked and Howard listened carefully.

On the next day Cochise took the white men on a tour of the Stronghold. Howard noted how good this place would be to defend. He saw that the chief had the makings of a first-rate general.

Then Cochise led them to a ridge from which they could look down on the camp, and outward over the mountains. He pointed with his lips, Indian fashion, to the huts from which the smoke was swirling. He swept his arm out in an arc, encompassing the blue mountains, the evergreens, the warmly-colored walls of cliffs.

"The *Americanos*," he said, "seem to have no homes. They are happy to go to any new place and live there. This is our home. This is where those who lived before us are buried. Here are the places where we may live in harmony with our gods. Here we, too, shall go to sleep when our time comes. Here our roots go into the ground and nourish our hearts. If we are driven away from here, we shall wither away and die."

Jeffords had already told General Howard how deeply the Indians loved their native land. The general had been surprised; he had always heard that wild Indians like the Apaches were rootless wanders. As he listened to the chief, he realized that Jeffords was right.

This fact might make negotiating more difficult. There were many whites who would object if the Chiricahuas were allowed to stay in their mountains. Many white men wanted the good grazing and the possible gold.

It was not until the seventh day of his visit that the general and the chief really got down to business. For the first six days they were taken up with getting to know each other. Both of them knew that trust in each other was all-important. Without that, negotiating was useless. On the seventh day they were ready.

It was already clear that Cochise wanted peace if he could get it under proper conditions. General Howard spoke of this. Then he spoke of the Warm Springs reservation, where the friends of the Chiricahuas, the Mimbreños, had been placed. He also mentioned the mountains that had been set aside for Cochise's old allies, the Mescaleros.

Cochise rejected both. He saw no reason why his people should give up their homeland. Moreover, if he agreed to that, his people would not follow him. It was out of the question.

Howard then agreed that the tribe should stay where it was. Cochise stated what he considered the boundaries of their country. After some talk the two men agreed on a large area. This area included the Chiricahua and Dragoon Mountains, and reached south from those to the Mexican border.

Then Cochise asked that the fort in the Pass be abandoned. Howard answered that this would be a mistake. His friend knew as well as he did that there were many bad men who would be glad to stir up trouble if they could. If trouble-makers came into the territory, and the Apaches killed them, then then there would be a great deal of anger. As long as troops were there, the trouble-makers would not dare to try anything. After some thought, Cochise agreed.

He said that his people must keep their weapons. They had not been conquered; they were not surrendering. They were making peace. They were putting themselves under the great chief in Washington, but they were doing this as free men. After a little talk, Howard accepted this. He saw it was a matter of pride. Also, if the Chiricahuas were allowed to keep their weapons, that proved that this peace was not a trap.

Now, Cochise told him, they came to the biggest thing of all. The chief, his friend, would return to the East. They must have someone with authority to stand by them and deal with the soldiers and the other *Americanos*. He said that he wanted nothing to do with the useless Indian Agents that were in the territory. He wanted a true friend, a man he could trust. There was only one such man, his nephew here.

When he had said this, Jeffords objected. He did not want to be an Indian Agent.

Cochise said, "Nephew, it is you who are making this peace happen. It has been your doing. There is no one else but you that we can trust. You have picked this peace up and you have been carrying it with you. You cannot let go of it. You cannot let it fall down and break."

Jeffords sat staring at the sky, thinking. General Howard asked, "What is it? Has something gone wrong?"

Jeffords answered, "No. Only I have a hard thing to decide." At length he sighed, and told Cochise, "I will do as you say." Then he interpreted to the general.

Howard said, "Excellent! You will receive your authority direct from the President. You will not be under the Indian Bureau or the War Department. You will be the President's agent. Thus you will have all the authority you need."

When that was settled, Cochise said, "Now I must take this to my people. I must call in my warriors and my chiefs who are away. I have twelve war parties out right now, making their livings. If I call them in, they must be able to come home in peace. I want you to go to your soldiers and have your chiefs call in the troops so that there will be no trouble."

Captain Sladen said that he could go. Cochise answered that the soldier chiefs might not listen to him. If his friend, this high chief, told them himself, then they would obey. Howard agreed to go.

The general set out the following morning with an escort of warriors. Captain Sladen and Jeffords, watching Howard go, remarked to each other that there was a sight you could hardly believe. The general in his uniform, with his white hair and beard and his fine carriage, rode as if he were at the head of an army of regulars. Behind him rode a dozen Apaches with painted faces.

Sladen said, "If some soldier sees that without knowing what it's all about, he'll think he's gone crazy."

CHAPTER XVII

WHILE THE GENERAL WAS away, there was an alarm that troops were coming to attack the Stronghold. Cochise offered to have Sladen and Jeffords taken to a distant hiding place, but both men had the courage and good sense to stay. This prevented Cochise from suspecting that the visit might have been a trap after all.

The attack did not take place, but Sladen watched how Cochise placed his men with great interest. When General Howard returned on the fourth day, the captain described what Cochise had done. Howard later reported that he knew of no officer who could have shown more skill in arranging a small group of men to fight off a superior force.

On the sixth day all the Chiricahuas were assembled. They gathered in council. The three white men, sitting on the edge of the circle, anxiously awaiting the decision, never forgot that occasion.

This matter was of grave importance. It would not do to start talking right away. First there had to be prayer. The women sang; then the men sang. The medicine men led them, shaking rattles to mark the time of the chants. When the prayers were over, many of the lesser chiefs got up and spoke in turn. Some were for peace, some were for war.

Finally Cochise arose. He made a long, impressive speech. He went over the terms of the agreement, and showed them the map that Howard had brought back with him. He told them what kind of a man this white-bearded soldier-chief was. Then he reminded his people how each year there were fewer Chiricahuas and more White-Eyes, and he told them to look into the future.

Finally, he said, "I stand here for peace. Let those who are with me stay here by me. If you all stay with me, or if I stand alone, I choose peace. Let those who want war move over on that side, by those rocks."

Eight or ten men got up and walked towards the rocks. When they saw how few they were, three of them turned back and sat down again. The others stayed firm.

Cochise said to them, "I am sorry that you will not stay with us. Since you have chosen war, war is for you. Take your families with you and ride into Mexico without turning aside. You are no longer Chiricahuas, and if my people meet you, they will fight."

The five men walked off.

When Jeffords had finished interpreting what had been said, the general heaved a deep sigh of relief. Cochise gestured to him then, and he went to join the chief.

In this way peace was made with the Chiricahuas. You might say that it was done by turning inside out the way in which Bascom had made the war. So long as Cochise and Jeffords lived, the peace remained unbroken and the Chiricahuas lived in their native land.

Not until many years later did other white men prove once more that they would not keep their word. With sudden force they drove the peaceful people out of their mountains and moved them, like prisoners, to a dreary, half-desert reservation far from their homes.

These white men who came later made the land that they stole in this way into a county, and later they named the county "Cochise." Somewhere there the chief is buried, no one knows where. Jeffords knew, but he never betrayed the secret. The bones of the great chief lie in peace in his native land, but possibly somewhere his soul knows that the peace he made was not kept to the end after all.

www.ingramcontent.com/pod-product-compliance
Lightning Source LLC
Chambersburg PA
CBHW020734020826
48980CB00016B/223